HARDSCRABBLE BOOKS

Fiction of New England

Laurie Alberts, *The Price of Land in Shelby*

Thomas Bailey Aldrich, *The Story of a Bad Boy*

Anne Bernays, *Professor Romeo*

Chris Bohjalian, *Water Witches*

Sean Connolly, *A Great Place to Die*

Dorothy Canfield Fisher (Mark J. Madigan, ed.), *Seasoned Timber*

Joseph Freda, *Suburban Guerrillas*

Castle Freeman, Jr., *Judgment Hill*

Ernest Hebert, *The Dogs of March*

Ernest Hebert, *Live Free or Die*

Sarah Orne Jewett (Sarah Way Sherman, ed.), *The Country of the Pointed Firs and Other Stories*

Kit Reed, *J. Eden*

Rowland E. Robinson (David Budbill, ed.), *Danvis Tales: Selected Stories*

Roxana Robinson, *Summer Light*

Rebecca Rule, *The Best Revenge: Short Stories*

Theodore Weesner, *Novemberfest*

W. D. Wetherell, *The Wisest Man in America*

Edith Wharton (Barbara A. White, ed.), *Wharton's New England: Seven Stories and* Ethan Frome

Thomas Williams, *The Hair of Harold Roux*

Other books by Castle Freeman, Jr.

The Bride of Ambrose and Other Stories (short stories)
Spring Snow: The Seasons of New England from The Old
Farmer's Almanac (essays)

JUDGMENT HILL

A NOVEL

Castle Freeman, Jr.

University Press of New England
Hanover & London

UNIVERSITY PRESS OF NEW ENGLAND
publishes books under its own imprint and is the publisher for
Brandeis University Press, Dartmouth College, Middlebury
College Press, University of New Hampshire, Tufts University, and
Wesleyan University Press

University Press of New England, Hanover, NH 03755
© 1997 by Castle W. Freeman, Jr.
Printed in the United States of America

5 4 3 2 1

Library of Congress Cataloging-in-Publication Data
Freeman, Castle, 1944–
Judgment Hill : a novel / by Castle Freeman, Jr.
p. cm. — (Hardscrabble books)
ISBN 0–87451–832–6 (cl : alk. paper)
I. Title. II. Series.
PS3556.R3838J83 1997
813'.54—dc21   97–8359

To
Alexander Chaffee Freeman
Sarah Snowden Freeman
this book is dedicated
with love

The king spake, and said, Is not this great Babylon, that I have built for the house of the kingdom by the might of my power, and for the honour of my majesty?

While the word was in the king's mouth, there fell a voice from heaven, saying, O king Nebuchadnezzar, to thee it is spoken: The kingdom is departed from thee.

And they shall drive thee from men, and thy dwelling shall be with the beasts of the field: they shall make thee to eat grass as oxen, and seven times shall pass over thee, until thou know that the most High ruleth in the kingdom of men, and giveth it to whomsoever he will.

—The Book of Daniel 4:30–32

PART I

South of White River the great highway, 91, takes a bend to the west on top of a rise, and as you go into it you can look over the country for twenty, thirty miles and see 91 where it winds and turns along the river valley, path of conquest, serpent, vast, corrupting worm, fell messenger, incubus—a soul-harlot lewdly lying beside the chaste green hills.

Right at the top of the rise, the highway builders have left a little pullout beside the southbound lanes, a promontory where you can stop and admire the country. Up there early on a morning at the beginning of June, Marvin Bland and Hugh, in Mr. Benteen's new Mercedes with Hugh driving and Marvin's dog riding in the rear, found the white car from the county sheriff's department waiting for them. Marvin stopped beside it and the deputy opened his door, got out, and came over. He opened the rear door of the Mercedes and got in the back with Marvin's dog.

"This Garrett's new rig?" the deputy asked. "What's he want something like this for?"

Hugh looked at Marvin. He grinned.

"The man has a certain style to keep up, Mr. Deputy," said Hugh. "He needs to show who he is, who you are. Cost you a month's pay to change the oil in this automobile. Remember that."

"Real cute, aren't you?" the deputy said. He looked carefully around the interior of the car. He ran his hand over the leather that covered the seats.

"Not too shabby," the deputy said. "Not too shabby. What would you have to give for a thing like this?"

Hugh looked at Marvin again.

"I don't know," he said. "What do you think, Marv? Couple of million? Fact is, Mr. Deputy, if you got to ask what it costs you can't afford it."

"So cute," the deputy said. "Well, he can have it. You know? Garrett, he can have it. What it is, all it is for him is a smooth ride to the nuthouse, the crazy house, far as I'm concerned."

"Least he'll be riding in style," said Hugh. "Your time comes, you'll be lucky if they give you that piece of shit Plymouth."

"Listen," the deputy said.

"I'm listening," Hugh said. "I'm listening to you. What?"

"Cut it out," said Marvin. "Cut it out, now. We got work to do. We ought not to be sitting around up here."

"You watch your mouth," the deputy said. "A mouth that big—"

"What?" said Hugh.

"Be careful. Just be careful."

"Careful?" said Hugh. "I'm always careful, Mr. Deputy. You know that."

"Someday you won't be," the deputy said. "Someday you'll drop it. I'll be there."

"Come on," said Marvin. "Cut it out. Where is she? Get her in here and let's go."

"See if you want her first," the deputy said. "She's different. I wish your mom had come," he said to Hugh. Hugh looked over at the deputy's white cruiser, at the young woman sitting in the back.

"What's the matter with her?" he asked.

"She's a piece of work," said the deputy. "Attitude on her, too. She acted like I was nothing but her driver, up here. Her driver, you know? What is that?"

"Her chauffeur," said Hugh. "Means she won't take your shit. Good for her. What's she look like?"

"She looks like about twenty-five dollars," the deputy said. "She's bad news. She's got a problem, too. I can take her right back, right now, if you want."

"What problem?" Marvin said.

"Her husband. Boyfriend. Whatever he is. He's in custody. They'll hold him thirty days, she says."

"What's after thirty days?"

"What do you think?" the deputy said. "He'll come looking for her. He's a piece of work, too."

"You know him?" Marvin said.

"Me? No. It's what she says."

"You believe her?"

"Yeah, I do," the deputy said. "Wait 'til you see her. Somebody busted her up pretty good."

"But you'll protect her, won't you, Mr. Deputy?" said Hugh.

"Not me," said the deputy.

"Well," Marvin said. "We'll take her. Cordie said okay. She'll want to talk to her, anyway."

"She don't want to get mixed up in this," the deputy said. "I'll take her back right now."

Marvin opened the door and got out of the car.

"Take her back where?" he said. "Come on. Let's have a look at her."

W̲ell, I saw from the first minute, before they were in the house, even, that she was something different, though how is another question. Not how I knew: how different. She had a bump on her head you could see all the way from the house, a bad one, but a lot of them have the same or worse. She wasn't different to look at, I mean: not a little girl, but not real tall. Hair light brown, a nice, kind of serious face. Nice smile. Big brown eyes.

Wide open, too. This one looked right at you, spoke right up. A lot of them don't have much left by the time they get here. They're about out of gas. She was different: not a whipped puppy but a dog that if you thrashed her would turn right around and take a piece out of you. Tough, I guess. A girl who can take care of herself, although probably not real well or else why is she here? Sometimes it's when they look most like they can that they most can't. Anyway, different for around here, where we generally just take it and shut up. My, my, I said to myself. Here is something new.

And didn't he know it, too? Wonder Boy. Carried her bag. Opened the door for her.

This is Miz McClellan. My mother, Mrs. Blankenship.

Looking at her like she's water in the desert. So taken that he almost managed to shut up and have manners and make sense. That's how taken. Uh-oh, I thought.

Tyler McClellan, she said. Standing there. Some of them fall all over you. Not her. I don't know how to thank you, she said.

Don't thank me 'til you know me, I said. Have you eaten breakfast?

Ummmm, he said to me. Can I talk to you a minute in the kitchen?

He wants to tell you about Hulon, she said. To warn you. Who's he?

A man, she said. He might be around.

Maybe you better tell me about him yourself, I said. Anyway, I said to him, don't you have work to do? You were haying, weren't you?

Top-of-the-woods, he said. We dropped Marv there on the way in.

6

You did? I said. He's up there. You're here. Who's with Garrett?

At that time we'd started to keep an eye on Garrett again, when we could. Not making a big thing of it. Just being careful.

I don't know, he said. He was at the inn having breakfast.

That's okay, then. I'm going over later, I said. You take Miz McClellan's case on up to her room and you get along.

I thought I'd stick around, he said. See if she needed any help settling in.

Git, I said.

He got.

So, I said to her. What about this—what's his name?

Hulon, she said. His name is Hulon.

"You want to go by the piece?" Marvin said to Hugh. "You can drop me."

Hugh got behind the wheel of Mr. Benteen's Mercedes with Marvin beside him. The young woman sat in back with her suitcase, a cardboard box full of more of her clothes, and Marvin's dog. They turned around in the pullout and got back onto the highway.

"What's that trooper's name?" the girl asked.

"Buddy Rackstraw," Hugh said. "He's a sheriff's deputy."

"What's the matter with him?" she asked.

"He's an asshole," Hugh said. "He thinks he's in a TV show."

"I mean," the girl said.

Hugh was looking at her in the rearview mirror as he drove.

"That's quite a bump you got," he said.

She touched the bruise above her right eye.

"I ran into a door."

"Right," said Hugh. "Buddy said your boyfriend did it. He said your boyfriend was coming after you when he got out of jail."

"He might," the girl said.

"I'm Hugh Blankenship," Hugh said. "You're going to be staying at my house. My mother's house. If your boyfriend's going to turn up we ought to know about it."

"Listen," the girl said, "if he turns up you'll know about it quick enough."

"Is there going to be trouble with him?" Hugh asked.

"I wouldn't be surprised," she said. "Hulon is mostly trouble."

"Is that his name?" Hugh asked. "Hulon?"

"Hulon Bear," the girl said.

"You're kidding," said Hugh. "What is he, some kind of Indian?"

"He says so."

"He's in jail?"

"He was last I saw him."

"But not in Brattleboro," said Hugh "You've been in Brattleboro. Where's he in jail?"

"Dallas."

"Dallas?" Hugh said. "Texas? He's in Texas? Shit, what are you worried about him for?"

"I'm not worried about him," the girl said. "You are."

"You're from Texas?" Hugh said. "What were you doing in Brattleboro?"

"Car died," the girl said.

"You were looking to put as much country as you could between you and old Hulon before he gets out," Hugh said.

"Something like that."

"Well," Hugh said. "You did pretty good."

Marvin hadn't spoken since they had left the deputy beside 91, but after they had gotten off the highway and onto the road that leads west into the hills, he said, "What's your name?"

"Tyler McClellan," the girl said.

"Tyler?" said Hugh. "That's quite a name. That's a Southern girl's name, I guess, right?"

"I guess," said the girl.

"Like Scarlett O'Hara," Hugh said. "They all got names like that," he said to Marvin. Marvin nodded.

"You can call me Rhett," Hugh said. "You see that movie?"

"Yeah," said Tyler McClellan.

"You remember where he carries her up the stairs?" Hugh said. "That was hot stuff back then, you know it? In those days, that was sexy."

"You thought so?" Tyler said.

"We got stairs at our house," Hugh said.

"You do?"

They left the road and entered a short dirt track that led through a belt of trees to a wooded lane and so uphill, bumping, to a gate in a stone wall. Beyond, a large open field. Hugh stopped the car short of the gate.

"Wait a minute," said the young woman, Tyler. "Wait. What's going on? What is this?"

"Bet she thinks we got her off in the woods, here, and now we're going to have our way with her," Hugh said. "Don't worry. We don't work that quick. You got to buy us a drink first, nibble our ear, you know? This old guy has got to get to work. This is his office."

He left the car and walked toward the gate. Tyler and Marvin and Marvin's dog waited for him. Tyler looked around them out the car's windows, front and rear. They were stopped in a silent green woods. The broad leaves of the trees ticked against the car, the old stone wall, tumbled down, went off through the woods to the right and left, ahead of them the big clearing, a hayfield, spread like a prairie, and beyond it and into the farthest distance the hills crowded away past sight: green, green, blue, gray.

"This is where we're going?" Tyler asked. "This is Amherst?"

"Ambrose," Marvin said. "North Ambrose. No. It's down there."

"Down where?"

"In the river valley. Three, I don't know, four more miles," Marvin said.

"What's there?" Tyler asked. "Ambrose. What is it?"

"It's a town," said Marvin.

"That's Ambrose, New York?" Tyler asked.

"Vermont," Marvin said.

"Where?"

"Vermont," Marvin said. "This is Vermont. You're in Vermont."

"Okay," said Tyler. "Vermont. Is that in New York?"

"Nowhere near," Marvin said.

"Shoot," said Tyler. "I ought to have been in New York. I was in New York, I know that. I was going to Canada."

"It's up there," Marvin said. "You didn't quite make it."

"I guess not," Tyler said. "Where, did you say?"

"Vermont," Marvin said. "Ambrose, Vermont."

"I'm staying there? In Ambrose? We're going there now?"

"You and him," said Marvin. "You leave me up here."

Hugh had opened the gate and was coming back toward them, walking in the lane.

"He thinks he's something, doesn't he?" Tyler said.

"Don't pay him too much mind," said Marvin. "He don't mean any harm. He's a kid's always been the smartest thing, the prettiest thing around."

"He is pretty," the girl said.

"Ain't he?" said Marvin.

Hugh came back and they drove through the gate and along the edge of the mowing to the tractor. Marvin had left the tractor up there. He got out of the car. His dog got out, too. The dog was a kind of buckskin-colored retriever, a placid dog, large, not young.

"He's a nice quiet old boy, isn't he?" Tyler said to Marvin. "What's his name?"

"His name? He's a dog. He don't have a name," Marvin said.

"He doesn't?" Tyler said. "Don't you have a name? He ought to have a name."

"No need," Marvin said. "There's only the two of us. He knows if I'm talking I'm talking to him."

"Come on up front with me, Miz Tyler," said Hugh. "We'll leave these two. We got another ten minutes to ride."

"I'm fine where I am," Tyler said.

"Oh, come on," said Hugh. "Get the view up here."

"I got it," Tyler said. "You drive, I'll ride."

"Suit yourself," said Hugh. He winked at Marvin standing beside the car. "Just like Buddy told it," Hugh said.

He backed the big car around in the grass to get it pointed to the gateway. He nodded to Marvin, who waited for them to drive away.

"Take care of that car," Marvin said to Hugh. "Garrett'll skin you, you nick it."

Hugh grinned.

"Fuck Garrett," he said. "I could bring it back on three wheels and Garrett would never know the difference and you know it."

It's true: she thought she was in New York. She had been in New York along of the day before, she knew that. She didn't know she'd left. Vermont I don't think she'd ever heard of for sure or if she had she didn't know it was a state, but maybe some other kind of place.

God's sake, I said to her. Didn't you go to school? Didn't they teach you the states? I know the schools today aren't up to much but I thought surely. In my day when you went to school you learned the states, the capitals, products. Course you might not learn a lot more . . .

I guess they taught them, she said. I guess I wasn't paying attention that day.

I guess you weren't, I said.

Canada. She had been on her way to Canada. She had under a hundred dollars and an old car that had had the course a long time ago, so Canada looked like about the best she could do. Never been out of Texas and she was a little hazy on just where Canada lay, too. She thought once you started seeing signs for Philadelphia you were pretty close and it seemed like she'd been driving an awful long time since then. On 91 coming into Brattleboro her car had started to put out black smoke. Then it had quit. She had spent two days in a motel. Then her money was gone and she couldn't pay the bill. She'd told the manager. He called the police. The police called the women's shelter down there. They called me.

Well, as it is, you nearly made it, I told her. Another couple of hours, no more. Canada was, I meant.

I just need a quiet place off the main roads. Because of Hulon, you see. When he gets out.

Wait a minute, I said. This Hulon. Are we talking about a husband here? Your husband, or just a boyfriend?

Boyfriend, I guess, she said.

You guess, I thought. Okay, I said, go on. But what I thought was: What did you expect? Whatever it is you are about to tell me, what did you expect? I don't mean to tell other people what's right and what's wrong, but some things, I don't care, you're asking for trouble. Asking for it. I know, I know: I'm a different generation. So I shut up. But so much of the trouble I see with the girls who come here is from them just dropping into and out of things with men, just dropping in and out.

Hulon says I'm the bride of Satan, she said. He can't marry me because I'm already married to Satan.

You are? I said.

Hulon was no prize. Half Indian and about the size of a tree to hear her tell it: six-six, six-seven. They were living in a trailer. Nothing wrong with that, I've lived in trailers, more than one. But with Hulon there were a lot of drugs, a lot of trouble of one kind and another. He hit her around, it was all connected with her being the bride of Satan. One time he'd thrown her across the trailer and she'd hit her head and got a concussion. She had seen double for three days. After that she decided the next time she'd shoot him. Hulon had a lot of guns. But what finally happened was he tied her to the bed in the trailer so she couldn't get out while he was gone, but she got loose and went down to the doughnut shop, not knowing that's where he'd gone. He grabbed her and tried to smash her head through the glass counter where they kept the chewing gum. They called the police. It took five policemen to get Hulon down and into the wagon, and afterward two of them went to the hospital. So Hulon was out of the picture but maybe not for long. She was meant to make a statement down there but she didn't wait around. By the end of the week she was in my kitchen. Some story.

She knew Hulon would be after her. He'd be let go the

end of June, unless he did something else she didn't know about. Then he'd be coming.

Listen, I said. You've come a thousand miles. He'll never find you. Probably he'll never even try.

Yes, he will, she said. He'd be after her. He was part Indian and those people never forget and never let go. Plus he was crazy, with his drugs and his bride of Satan business. He handled snakes. Serpents, she said. He handled serpents. Oh, he'd try to run her down. And the thing was, she was still friends with Hulon's mom and she'd told her she was heading north. She'd tell Hulon when he got out. She wouldn't want to, but he'd make her. Then he'd be on her track.

Well, I said, you didn't tell him you were coming this way, did you?

No, she said, she hadn't known which way she was going, just north.

He won't find you just by going north, I said. Where's he going to look?

You haven't seen Hulon, she said.

Maybe not, I said, but let me tell you something I have seen. I've seen it again and again. I've had over two dozen girls come through here, stay here, for weeks, for longer, to get away from some man. Just like you. With every one of those girls the man was supposed to be after her. He was looking for her, he was going to find her and drag her out of here, take her back. But not a single time did any man ever turn up. Never. And I'm talking about girls from here: Brattleboro, the Falls, White River. Nobody came for them, even from that close. Do you see what I'm saying? Do you think some guy is going to come all the way from Texas to here when they won't make the trip from White River? I'm not worried.

He'll be here, she said.

Well, maybe, maybe not. These girls who come here, to

tell the truth, half of them are let down when the men they think they're hiding from don't find them, don't even try. The fact is, those men couldn't care less, they have long since found some other girl to beat up on.

Not him, she said. Not Hulon. Hulon will come.

Mr. Benteen, W. Garrett Benteen, with his proprietary eye, walked through the woods. His woods. Whose woods were these he knew damned well: they were his. Every tree, every flower, every rock of them belonged to him. Ahead, beyond the trees, was the round thirty-acre hayfield they called top-of-the-woods. He owned it, too. From top-of-the-woods you could see over to the neighboring place, also his, as was the farm adjoining it farther down the valley toward the village, as was the one after that. Benteen owned them all. He farmed them all, farmed them, anyway, in a manner of speaking.

A kind of farm. A farm for our time.

There are in old Vermont today other husbandmen like Benteen, more of them than you might think. All are farmers of a kind, in that their occupation is the earth's increase. They make milk, beef, wool, mutton, lumber, pulp, Christmas trees, maple syrup, and so on. Nor are they by any means the worst farmers in the state, nor are they the least dedicated.

And yet . . . and yet.

For the fact is, these are farmers whose agriculture is based not only on the earth's increase but also, and essentially, on a regular and abundant harvest of high-quality com-

mercial paper, government obligations, corporate shares, and other like instruments. They may reap from the land, but they sow elsewhere and otherwise. There is a fat feather bed between their bones and the price of hogs.

They are a quiet bunch, the rich farmers. They look like every other farmer (unless, like Benteen, they look worse, much worse). They don't go in for show. From that, and from the fact that the good or ill fortune of their husbandry depends on forces remote from the farm itself, it happens that their presence and magnitude may be revealed in odd ways. When in the fall of 1987, for example, Wall Street missed a beat or two, panic and doom descended on these hills far to the north with the cruelty of a killing frost in June. Following on a fictitious reversal of fictitious gains on indexes not one man in fifty who follows them really understands, the destruction among the gentry of Vermont was nevertheless frightful. Tree farmers leapt from high boughs. Shepherds fell on their crooks. Maple sugar makers drowned themselves in their holding tanks. Beekeepers flung themselves on their hives and were stung to death.

No, not really.

Not really. Nor was Mr. Benteen much affected at the time. He had good advice. And anyway he knew very well that his own wealth that came and went in cities was perfectly imaginary. That was its safety: you can't destroy what has no reality. What was not imaginary was not in the markets, exchanges, banks, but right here. It was the land, the serried hills, steeple-pierced, wood or meadow or planting, plowland and hayland, brook and pond, the country in its pitch and breadth extending before you mile after mile. There was nothing unreal about it. You could touch it, see it, hold it, smell it, be born onto it, be buried in it—and therefore you could lose it. You could watch it diminish, erode, corrupt, waste quite away.

A country in transition. In transition.

He followed the grass-grown rutted track that led to the barway opening on top-of-the-woods. Over his head songbirds and squirrels were busy in the branches, and now as he walked, a partridge sprang apparently from under his descending foot and spun off into the woods with a loud noise like a flail. Mr. Benteen went steadily on. He carried a pair of binoculars around his neck on a cord, but it wasn't birds he was looking to watch today. Ahead the woods parted.

Benteen knew that by now he ought to have heard the clacking and racking of the mower, but instead the sound that came from the opening was an irregular banging of metal on metal. They must be broken down.

Bank, bank, clank, bink came from the clearing, aimless. It must be Hugh up there.

Benteen stopped at the edge of the woods and looked out over the mowing. They had been around seven, eight times, no more. Hugh, the tractor, and the cutter bar were fifty feet from him, opposite the barway where he stood. Hugh's back was to him. He was beating on the hitch, or maybe on the cutter itself, with a hammer. Marvin Bland was nowhere to be seen.

Benteen walked across the mown band to Hugh. He walked on the fresh-cut hay lying deep in rows, alive and springing. He had to pick up his feet, lift his knees high, like a deer, and go slowly. Benteen walked through the new hay the way you walk in a dream.

Hugh saw him when he came near. He gave the cutter one last shot with his hammer (*bink*), to show Benteen—well, to show him something.

"Motherfucker," said Hugh to the cutter.

"That's pretty," said Benteen. "Where did you learn to talk like that? You talk like a nigger."

"Movies," said Hugh.

"They don't talk like that in the movies," said Benteen. "They're not allowed."

"What's the last movie you been to?" Hugh said.

"Where's Marv?"

"Gone back to get the tools. Thing won't unhitch."

"Why unhitch it?"

"Marv wants to quit. He says it's going to rain."

Benteen looked up into the sky. From top-of-the-woods you could see off to the west. He saw no rain up there. A few small clouds high in the south. The sun, halfway through the afternoon, had a clear path to the western horizon. There was a little breeze that came and went. The air had a summer smell: dust and grass, dust and grass.

"Look at that," said Benteen. "It's not going to rain. Smell the air. What makes him think it's going to rain?"

"He heard it on the radio," said Hugh.

"The hell he did," said Benteen. "Look at that sky. You tell him when he gets back I'll give him a dime for every drop that drops the rest of today and tomorrow too."

"I'll tell him," Hugh said. "What are you doing up here? You got your glasses. Who are you spying on?"

"Condostas will be starting across the brook," Benteen said. "I'm keeping an eye on them. There's a place over here where you can see the whole job."

"So what?" Hugh said. "What's to see? Terry in his new hat, walking around trying to look like he knows what he's doing? Why? What kind of game is that?"

"It's no game," said Benteen. "You think that's a game over there? That's no game."

"Sure," said Hugh. "Listen: think you could help out a little here? If you were to get up on that hitch and kind of bounce it up and down, maybe I could get the fucker to let go."

"Bounce it up and down yourself," said Benteen. "What do I pay you for?"

Hartshorne, Singletary, Nightingale, Hatch.

Dana, Mackenzie, Blankenship, Patch.

It's like a song, isn't it? Or, no: it's a fucking nursery rhyme. You drive through the village, the houses, their owners, one after the other, you're driving through a nursery rhyme. The worst of it is, it's a nursery rhyme you're in: you're part of the song. The worst of it is, everybody else is in it, too, and everybody knows the same words. Everybody knows you. They know all about you. You about them.

Hartshorne, Singletary: a widow and a drunk, then a total fucking jerk and another drunk. Dana, Mackenzie: a nutcase, a religious fanatic, and Patch a what do you call it? Whose wife screws everybody in the state?

Cuckold.

Blankenships, the same: another widow. Her boy, too bad. Big disappointment. Bright. Sent to college, big opportunity. Generosity of a kind friend. Friend, did you say? Say, benefactor. Say, boss. Anyway, big opportunity for the kid. (They don't have a dime.) What did he do with it? He blew it. Fucking blew it off. And now where is he? What's he doing?

Well, doing some better lately. How about that cowgirl, that Yellow Rose, that Calamity Jane, that Debbie Does Dallas. How about her? Too beat up, you say? Hell, no. What about that bruise? Well, what about it? That's character's what that is, and anyway, can't be too particular about the material at Cordie's Home for Unfortunate Females, can we? We're talking about hurt goods, there. In that crowd Debbie is looking fine. You betcha.

Came to the right place, too. See the old bat suck her in there? Fucking Electrolux. She loves anything she can boss around. She'll put her in the end room upstairs, get her a job making beds at the inn, fix her up for life, run her life. And if her killer boyfriend shows up she'll sit him right down in the kitchen and begin explaining things—town, herself, me, the weather, the inn, the neighbors—and in fifteen minutes the poor bastard will run screaming from the house and not stop 'til he's back in Texas. So she's safe from him.

There is that, too: safe. Safety. It's all there when you need it. Hartshorne, Singletary, Nightingale, Hatch—all of them. The whole nursery rhyme. It's there when you need it. Dana, Mackenzie, Blankenship, Patch. Thing is, it's also there when you don't. It's always there. It's always the same. Towns like this is like having the same job all your life. Or, no: towns like this is like the Mafia: you can't join, but you can't quit. If you're in you can't get out. Try and they'll drop you into cement, you end up in an overpass on 91. What we need for places like this is a deal like where they sneak you out of town and relocate you to California. You get a new name, new job, bank account. New life. That's the only way you can get out. Witness protection. Yeah, I'm in the Vermont Witness Protection Program, here. Which way to Beverly Hills?

Splat, plop. Look. *Plop, splat.* I love it. Old Marv right on the money. Heard it on the radio. *Plop.* A dime a drop? A dime a drop, I think you said? *Plop.* Pay me. Pay me, you stupid, blind motherfucker. I'm eating your lunch and you don't even know it. And if you don't like the way I talk you can insert it right up to the handle and turn it clockwise.

Across the Dead River branch, here about thirty feet wide, they were getting ready. The branch was Mr. Benteen's line. He watched them through his binoculars from the woods at the top of the hill opposite. There were two pickup trucks and a sedan parked along the road, and six men: Marco Condosta, his son, Terry, in his cowboy hat, a man Benteen didn't know, and three choppers. The choppers were working along the road in the brush. Benteen heard their saws start up. Marco and the man Benteen didn't know had a map spread out on the hood of the sedan. Terry had gone ahead into the woods past where the choppers were working.

The choppers were making the yard. They would clear, oh, a quarter-acre. Marco did nothing by halves. He'd have an engineer in—well, that would be what the other man was, Marco's engineer. He'd clear yard enough to muster an army, then he'd make the skidder roads up the hill into the trees, the condemned woods, the doomed woods. The roads he'd lay out fair, he'd drain them, he'd bring in gravel if he had to. Marco would work fast, once he got in there. He would bring in all the men he needed and a couple more, all the equipment and some over. The affair would go off like an invasion, but perfectly: an invasion of a stronghold without defenders. With only one defender.

Here they come. This is no drill.

What was up there? Fifty acres, seventy-five, steep enough at the bottom, less steep as you went up. Bears and owls and porcupines. An old farm lane, grown up to woods, stone walls either side, stone walls lying through the woods over the whole hillside. One cellar hole that Benteen knew about, probably more he hadn't found. Good pines below, and higher, maples and oaks, some of them big, some enormous. Floors and spoons and clothespins and toothpicks.

Otherwise it's not a real thing. It's a game.
It's no game. This is no drill.

Mr. Benteen lowered his glasses. Below, on the road that lay beside the branch, Hugh in his hot red car came down toward the parked trucks and the men. Hugh had a used sports model with a oversized engine, a faulty muffler, and poor brakes—not unlike its driver, in fact. He beeped at Marco and the engineer as he blew past, beeped again, waved, and fired on down the road toward the village, headed home. Marvin must have come for him. They had quit mowing, then. Benteen wondered if Marvin really had feared rain. Hugh might have made that up so he could quit early. But then where had Marvin been? In any case they were finished for today.

He turned and started back through the woods toward the mowing and the track down to the house. Behind him the noise of the choppers' saws went on and on, rising and falling, a drone that rose from Condosta's choppers and from a thousand, ten thousand more, rose from the woods up and down the hills like mingled voices, like song, like prayer.

Hugh's father had been a small man and never strong, but nobody knew him to be ill. He worked for Mr. Benteen, too. One day in that same time of the year he and Marvin Bland had been haying. About noon Hugh's father had said he didn't feel at all smart. They quit for lunch. Marvin told him to sit down in the shade while Marvin went for the water jug.

When Marvin came back with the water, he found Hugh's father sitting in the grass dead. He'd had a bad heart, somehow, all along.

Hugh had been three then. There was no money, none at all, not a dime. His mother, Cordelia, had taken him and moved back in with her own mother in Dead River Settlement, in the southern part of the town. She had lost her father only the year before.

Cordelia didn't get on with her mother, never had, so within two months she and Hugh were back in the village in the house her husband had rented from Mr. Benteen. She went to work at the Benedict House as a chambermaid. She had never in her life before worked for wages. In a year she was running the inn's three housekeepers. In two years she was running them and the kitchen as well. In three years she was running the whole place. She didn't marry again. She said nobody she knew would have her, but no doubt the real reason was she didn't need to take on another husband now that, with the inn, she had plenty to run as it was.

Hugh at first was a small boy with fine yellow curls who stuck close to his mom. The worry was that he was flawed, obscurely weak, like his father. Then when he turned twelve he started to grow. He reached six feet before he was sixteen and was sound and solid, though his hair remained as fair and soft as it had been in childhood and so at twenty-two he looked like an overgrown cherub, a sugar angel in the too-tight, handed-down uniform of a small-town high school football player.

"Good one, too," Cordelia told Tyler McClellan. "He played for Little River Union. He and Terry Condosta from town, here. Then they both went on to Dartmouth and played there. Dartmouth: that's not like some poor little country college, you know. That's the real thing. He was an A student, too, at least in school. Believe it or not."

"Was?" Tyler said.

"Was. He left after football season his freshman year. He came home."

"Why?"

"They kicked him out."

"Kicked him out? What did he do?"

"About everything you can do, I guess," said Cordelia. "Terry finished up okay. Graduated last year. He's here working for his father, doing very well."

"Well, maybe your boy could go back some time."

"They'd never have him," Cordelia said. "He's got what you might call a temper. He got in a fight with one of the coaches. Put him in the hospital. That was kind of the last thing. They called me and I said I'm not surprised to hear from you. I expected your call, I said. I called Garrett, then, because Garrett had been paying his bills up there. I'm not surprised, I told Garrett. And he said, Well, I am. Oh, really? I said. Yes, Garrett said. This is February. I thought he'd be out by Thanksgiving."

"Well," said Tyler. "A boy I knew? A boy I knew like that went in the Air Force."

"That wouldn't be a real good idea for him," said Cordelia. "He has kind of a hard time with authority, you could say. Like that you can't fly? That you have to open the door before you go through the wall? That two apples and two apples make four apples, not six, not a hundred dollars? Those are his idea of authority.

"Well, he works for Garrett, now, mostly on the big place, but wherever he needs him. Garrett don't drive. Hugh drives him around. And then, Marvin always needs hands. It's outside work, farm work. You know. Mainly he helps Marvin out."

"I met Marvin," Tyler said. "He's the one with the dog."

"Marvin?" Cordelia said. "He's like Garrett's foreman, I guess. Garrett figures out what he wants to get done, tells Marvin, Marvin sees to it. And then when Garrett forgets to figure out what he wants to get done, Marvin remembers and does it on his own.

"Marv's all right. He's straight. No ball of fire, though. I guess you could tell that. Not a real champion. Marvin just does his job, always has. He must be, goodness, he was up ahead of me in school. He must be past fifty. He's getting to be an awful old bachelor, too.

"Hugh is terrible on Marvin," she said. "He calls him the monk, you know. Like a hermit? *He don't talk*, Hugh says. *He don't talk, and he don't walk, and he don't*—you know. He's after Marv all the time. Marv don't let it get to him. He just goes about his business. Marv's good with him."

"Hugh is real cute," said Tyler.

"I know it," said Cordelia. "The thing is, so does he. That's what Garrett says: he knows he's cute. That's the whole thing. Well, you're here now. You'll see for yourself."

"Who's Garrett?" asked Tyler.

"We talked about this," Marco Condosta said. "We talked about this before."

"Years ago," Mr. Benteen said. "You weren't thinking about it then. Now you are. You're getting ready to go in there."

"Tomorrow or the next day," Condosta said.

"You know what you'll get out, then," Benteen said. "You know to the penny. What's your best number? Tell me. I'll add thirty percent. I'll take it all. I'll take the whole hill. We can do it all this afternoon."

"I'd be robbing you," Condosta said. "You don't want it.

Believe me. Besides, it's my boy's thing. It's Terry's thing. I'm semiretired. I let him work on it, see what he can do, you know what I mean? He's a college boy, he doesn't know what he can do. I keep out of his way. Talk to Terry."

"It's his thing," Benteen said. "But who holds the land? Who owns the land—him, or you?"

"Me," Condosta said. "What do you think?"

"Then you can sell it," said Benteen.

"I told you," Condosta said, "it's up to Terry. Talk to Terry."

"I can't talk to Terry," Benteen said. "Terry's a kid. He doesn't understand."

"You're right about that," said Marco Condosta. He smiled sadly at Benteen and rapped the blotter on his desk with his knuckles. "You know what I paid for that land?" he asked.

"Not yet," Benteen said.

"Nine dollars an acre," Condosta said. "What a crime, you know? Nineteen forty-six, right after the war. I bought from Milo Tavistock. Remember Milo? He hated to sell to a dago. He told me so. But he had to because I met his price. Nine dollars. He made me buy his sugarhouse, too, down the other side. I had no need for it but I bought it anyway, all set up, all the equipment. You know for what? Another ten bucks. Not quite a thousand dollars in all. Milo thought he was so smart. He thought he was screwing me. The taxes on it every year are double that now, more than double. You know what I'm saying?"

"Then sell it," Benteen said.

"You must be crazy," Condosta said. "I won't rob you. It's no good up there. It's steep. It's wet. Springs. They can't work fast. I get done, I'll lose money up there. I'm only going in there to keep the mill busy. It's not business. It's not a real thing, you know what I mean? It's just for the mill."

"Why keep it, then?"

"I don't know," Condosta said. "Why buy it?"

"It's on my line," Benteen said. "I don't like to see it all cut down."

"Don't look," said Condosta. "You don't like to see it, don't look. You know what I'm saying?"

"You're not making sense," Benteen said. "You're a businessman. I'm offering you thirty percent over your best cut, before you start. How are you being smart to turn that down?"

"Smart?" said Condosta. "I'm not smart. I'm dumb. I'm a logger, you know what I mean? I run a sawmill. I came up here out of the army with a hundred bucks and an old Ford V-8. Nineteen forty-six. June, like now. June, nineteen forty-six. I wore my uniform pants for a year because they were all I had. I did okay because I stuck to what I started."

"You did okay because everybody was moving to New Jersey and building little houses out of two-by-fours, and up here the old men were selling out for nothing," Benteen said.

"Sure," said Condosta. "Sure, they were selling out. Sure, they were building. Why wouldn't they? People have got to live someplace, don't they? Listen, I know what you're saying, here. I don't like to see it all cut down, either. Nobody does. But that's the way it is. It's a crop. It's a commodity. You buy it, you sell it, you use it. Otherwise it's not a real thing, it's a game, like. You know what I'm saying?"

"It's no game," Benteen said.

"Yeah, it is," Condosta said. "But either way, we're going in. Put away your money. I don't want it. I got more money than I want. I bet you wouldn't think I'd say that. It's true. I got more than I wish I had. I'll tell you, though, talk to Terry. I'm semiretired. I told him it's his thing to do. Let him see what he can do. He won't go for it either, though, what you want."

"I wouldn't ask him," Benteen said.

"No," said Condosta. "You know, I don't see you from one year to the next. A little place like we got here and I never see you. You want some coffee? I'll get her to bring us some coffee. Charlotte?"

The Benedict House, a hotel, took up one side of the village square. The inn, it was called—sometimes the Ambrose Inn. It was a long brick building, two full stories with a dormered roof. Its dedication, in 1829, had been celebrated with large oratory by Daniel Webster, still the most perfect United States senator God ever struck off and a man who made a considerably better thing out of his time at Dartmouth College than had some of his successors.

The building had been put up to be a court and county house at a time when the village was the county seat. Only a few years after its completion, however, the county seat had been moved to another town more easily reached by road and rail. The courthouse had been given up, then, but a local man, Orestes Benedict, had bought the place proposing to run it as a hotel. In the 150 years following, the building had had at least seven lives: as a hotel, a school, a hotel again, communal living quarters for a religious order, hotel for the third time, repertory theater, and hotel yet again. Nevertheless, in spite of the variety of uses to which it had been put, the old place had most often and most happily existed as an inn, its success in that condition being demonstrated by its list of distinguished guests, a list that included the Marquis de Lafayette, Charles Dickens, U. S. Grant, Mark Twain, Rudyard Kipling, and Miss Bette Davis.

By now the place had been an inn for forty years. It had seventeen guest rooms (although three or four of them were usually rented as apartments by permanent residents of the place), a good kitchen, two gloomy parlors, a bar, and a long, lugubrious dining room. The present owner ran the place on the basis that food need not be tarted up as long as there was plenty of it; a room that has a real fireplace need not be spacious, or freshly painted, or even entirely clean; October is when you live or die; and, after all, you make your money on the booze.

The bar opened at five. The barman was Tom Tavistock, called Boomer, a stout boy a little older than Hugh, with a level gaze and a long ponytail. He was learning to be a cook.

"So, is your new roomer, ah, settled in there okay, is she?" Boomer asked Hugh.

"Oh, yeah," said Hugh.

"Perfectly comfortable, is she? Finding everything she needs now?"

"Everything," said Hugh.

"Happy to be there, is she?" Boomer asked.

"Says she is. Acts like she was."

"Does she?" Boomer asked. "That's good. That's good to know. How about you? You look kind of stretched out, man. Tired. I noticed when you came in, you're walking kind of funny, aren't you? Kind of bent over? Favoring your middle a little?"

"Must be it's a bad back," Hugh said.

"Must be that's it," said Boomer. "What should I get you, here?"

"How's the draft?" Hugh asked him. "Good and flat to-day?"

"Like always, man," Boomer said.

"Well, B., you can pull me one out," said Hugh.

Boomer brought a glass from under the bar and began to draw the beer.

"Though it's true I have been short of sleep," said Hugh. Boomer put the beer on the bar in front of him.

"Is that right?" he asked. "Last week or so, huh?"

"In there, yeah," said Hugh. "Can't understand it."

"Not good to go without your sleep, man," said Boomer. "It wouldn't have to do with that new roomer we were talking about, would it?"

"How could it, B.?" Hugh asked.

"Well," Boomer said. "One thing and another."

"You mean, like, her playing her radio too loud at night?"

"That kind of thing," said Boomer.

"She don't have a radio, B.," Hugh said.

"Is that right?" said Boomer. "Must be something else, then."

"I think you like her, B.," said Hugh. "I do. I think you'd like to take her downtown, wouldn't you?"

"No, man," said Boomer. "Not her. Not me. Too much baggage with her for me."

"How do you mean, baggage, B.?" Hugh asked.

"Well," said Boomer. "You heard about her old man."

"Everybody's heard about him," said Hugh. "So what?"

"She tell you he killed a man one time?" Boomer asked. "She saw it. He killed him with a sledgehammer, man."

"Come on, B.," said Hugh. "Why's he running around loose, then?"

"It was a Mexican he killed," Boomer said. "It don't count down there if it's a Mexican."

"Come on," said Hugh.

"No, it's true," said Boomer. "You don't know what it is down there. I've been, man. In the service. El Paso. They're all crazy down there. There are any amount of guys like her old man down there. I wouldn't touch her with a pole, just because of him."

"You worry too much, B.," Hugh said.

"He's coming," Boomer said. "She said he is, and he is.

When he does you don't want to be around her, anywhere near. I'm being serious now, man. I'm not shitting with you, here. She tells me. You best leave her alone. There are other girls."

"There are?" said Hugh. "There are? Here? Name two."

"You know what I mean, man," said Boomer.

"Them other ones don't live down the hall, B.," said Hugh. "They don't wash their tits in your sink. They don't take their showers in your bathroom."

"Kind of a target of opportunity, what you might call her, is she?" said Boomer.

"That's it, B.," said Hugh. "That's what she is. And anyway, suppose that sledgehammer fella does come on up? You and me could take him. We got sledgehammers up here, too, don't we? I know there's one out at Garrett's someplace. Big sucker, twelve-pound head. Maybe it's in the barn, I'll have to look. We could take him, right?"

"Wrong, man," said Boomer.

Go, then, I'd tell him. If it's so bad, go.

With all his moaning and groaning about town, here: it's so stupid, it's so boring, there's nothing to do, there's nobody to do it with. On and on. Everybody's a moron, the ones who aren't crazy. He's afraid he'll go crazy himself if he has to stick around much longer.

Don't, then, I said. If it's so bad, go someplace else. You're not a prisoner, you know. You got money saved.

Not much, he said.

Not much, I said. Not much, is right. Well, if it's all that bad, why didn't you not get yourself kicked out of Hanover?

That was worse, he said.

Well, I said, save your money. You don't have enough? Save 'til you do.

The way Garrett pays? he said. You don't know what you're talking about.

Well, I said, then get another job.

Doing what? he said.

See, there's always something, some reason.

Well, I guess that's up to you, I said. Hating it around here as much as you do, bored as you are, I'm sure you'll come up with something.

I'm working on it, he said.

You are? I said. Working on what?

Nothing, he said.

Well, it hasn't been easy for him. Never having a father around, another man. All these poor girls in and out of here. It can't have been easy. Marvin, I thought, they're close. No, they aren't. He thinks Marv's a joke. Well, he is. *He don't talk and he don't walk, and he don't—.*

Garrett, too. Garrett paid his way to Hanover. Garrett pays his wages right now. But Garrett's not the one. Garrett's kept his end of the deal. No, it was up to me, and I did my best and here we are. And if it comes to that, maybe he didn't miss all that much. I never heard of a boy who got on with his father: it's not in nature. My own Daddy always said, A boy's best friend is his mother. Kind of sing it, he would:

A boy's best friend is his mother.
No other.

I saw her light. Two o'clock in the morning, I saw the light under her door. Opened the door, there she is sitting on the bed, nothing on her. I mean nothing. She's naked. No nightie, no nothing. Looking at me. Not looking at me. Looking at I don't know. Looking.

And I thought, *Thank you, Jesus.* But then I thought, *Whoa* . . . Because no, she doesn't see me. She's way off. What's the matter with her?

What's the matter? I said. She just shook her head, didn't say anything.

So, shit, no. Not this way. I started to shut the door, get out of there.

Wait, she said.

Like that.

Not your regular waif, no. Not your ordinary unfortunate. Since I was old enough to know they were here they've been moving in and out, beat up, in tears, in shock, stunned dumb, closed down, like people in a car wreck. Like a dog in the pound that's been kicked. They get here and for a week they like hide under the furniture. Some don't even eat.

But Mom, she takes them in hand. Don't she just? She sits them in the kitchen. With her, never alone. They're with her all the time, in the kitchen, or over at the inn, or shopping, or watching TV. She gives them coffee. Fucking gallons of coffee, rivers. It works. Pretty soon they start to breathe. First thing you know, they're taking showers all the time. Baths. Three, four a day. Between the coffee bills and the hot water bills, it looked like I'd had to go off to school through the ice and snow without any shoes. Boo-hoo.

Yes, I'd check them out. Sure. It ain't hard, they're in and out of the shower all the time, they're in their rooms and the door don't close all the way. I've seen them, all sizes and shapes, big ones, little ones. I've seen bumps, scars, bruises, tattoos. That's right, tattoos.

Course they know I'm here too, and men are not exactly what they're into at this particular time of their lives. Not high on their lists of favorite things. No. So they're looking at me like I'm half the kid who delivers the groceries and half fucking Ted Bundy.

And then even when they're settled down, even when they're ready to move on, they're not right. They're not right in the head. They're suspicious. Or, no: they're frighty, like a dog that's been kicked and never forgets it no matter what happens to it after, like a gun-shy dog. Skittish.

Who needs that? Who needs getting looked at like a poisonous insect, like something low but evil? Not me. I can say truthfully that none of her Unfortunate Females ever much did it for me, I never wanted to take the trouble. So when you say, Well, what about that Debbie Does Dallas, what's that you're doing with her? I have to say, I know, I'm as surprised as you are. All I can tell you is she's not your regular waif.

I'd like to meet the guy that made her run. What's his name, Exxon? He's supposed to be something fucking else. That bump he gave her. I hope he does come after her. I hope he does show up here. I'd like to meet him, then I'd like to tear his lungs out and piss in the hole. I would, too.

Not your ordinary unfortunate, not by a long shot. Those waifs. I used to think they were my sisters, you know, when I was little? I used to think I had all these sisters. They aren't my sisters. They're nothing like me. There is no way I would let myself get treated like them. Never. I guess they get into something and then they can't get out, they just go on hoping it won't get worse. Course it always does. Waifs.

Not me.

Marvin shut off the engine and waited. The chatter of the cutter bar stopped. He sat and let the field all around him resume its silence. Not silence. He wasn't far from the end of the mowing and he could hear a little wind in the top of the pine trees. Below him, too, somewhere in the woods in the direction of the village, a bunch of crows kept up a squawking and cawing. And all around, the ticking of the cut hay.

On his right Marvin's dog moved out ahead of the tractor through the mowing. He went toward the woods a little way, trotting, his legs stiff, his head up. There were deer moving through the trees in there, just into the woods. Marvin watched the dog. The dog stopped, sat on his haunches. He saw them.

Three, four, five. They moved in no hurry through the little trees inside the woods. Even though they were not fifty feet from Marvin and were moving, still they were hard to see; they seemed not to take the light, or to take up all the light, like fish in a pool. They're right there but you can hardly see them. But if you waited you could.

There were two little ones, three bigger. One of the bigger ones might be a spike. Marvin tried to see. The deer picked their way idly among the trees. They never started or seemed to know he was watching them, but they never quite let him have a good look at them, either. They kept the little trees between.

The racketing crows passed overhead, their cries came down to him lazily.

Then something else. Something else in there, following the deer, but farther into the woods: dark and big. More than big.

Marvin's dog saw it, too. He stood up and froze, then ran

toward the woods, barking. The deer scattered. The other thing in there stopped, turned its head toward the dog. The dog, running, stopped short. His barking went up in pitch: *Yow, yow, yow. Yip, yip, yip.* He hadn't bargained on anything that size. He sat at the edge of the woods and yipped. Marvin stayed on the tractor. He saw it, too.

In a minute Marvin's dog came back to the tractor. He looked at Marvin and shook his head.

"Where do you think he came from?" Marvin asked the dog. "What do you think he's doing here?"

Am I blind, do they think? Am I deaf? Or am I just stupid? Do I not hear him sneaking down the hall in the middle of the night? Every night? Do I not see how he'd liked to wash himself away from all the time he spends in the shower? Do I not smell the stuff he's started to wear?

Do I believe he came home at ten A.M. the day I forgot my puzzle book and had to go back for it because he hurt his knee?

Do I like it? Not much. Well, all the girls that have come in and out of here, I suppose it was bound to happen sooner or later. Maybe it happened before. But with her, how am I supposed to like it? Her being different, not from around here at all, with a crazy man chasing her? And him with his smart mouth and all his brains has no more sense in his whole head than he has in what she leads him around by. Did I say that?

I like her. She's a nice kid. She's a good worker, too. I like having her around the house. Another woman in the house.

It was like I'm just the housekeeper for him. But now it's two against one, kind of, and I like that even though I don't always know who's the two and who's the one.

No, I like her. But she is something different. She's not thinking about him. She doesn't know what's going to happen to her. If it was some little girl in high school here, if it was one of the girls at the inn, you'd know what was on her mind. You'd know what she knew was coming. You'd know her whole life, better than she did.

Not with this one. She don't know. She's not thinking about him. She's thinking about taking care of herself. She's thinking about her boyfriend looking for her. She is trouble.

And if I'm honest I also know that if she weren't, if she weren't trouble, if there were no boyfriend, still she's not from here. She won't stay here. She'll be on her way some one of these days. So how am I to like it that they have, uh, started in, knowing it won't stay the same, can't stay the same? She'll take off and he won't. Or he will. Either way is wrong.

So, do I like it? Not much. Am I going to do something about it, then? No. I don't like it, and I'm watching. I won't stand for bad behavior but I also don't see starting a fight I can't win. What was it Daddy called that?

Bad generalship.

Cordelia put Tyler at the front desk. She made her her chatelaine. Tourists and other travelers arriving at the inn didn't like to walk into an empty hall. They wanted someone to meet them and tell them, once again, where they were. Therefore Cordelia got a dress for Tyler from one of the dining room girls and put her out front. Many evenings she had nothing to do. Then she would go through the door behind the desk into the bar and there, if Boomer was also idle, she would sit at the end of the bar and talk to him. She'd talk and talk. She would pour into Boomer's ready ear the burning, steaming infusion of her past.

"Then when he's done he bites their heads off," Tyler said.

"Bites their heads off?" Boomer asked. "Bites the snakes' heads off?"

"Bites them right off."

"Jesus," Boomer said. "Why?"

"He says it's part of his struggle," Tyler said. "With Satan? He picks them up, holds them, has them crawl all over him. These are Texas rattlers, now, three, four feet long. They're all around his neck, over his body, even down his pants. He handles them."

"I heard of that," Boomer said.

"It's from the Bible," Tyler said. "And then he'll bite their heads off because he says they have taken on the evil. What am I going to do if he comes?"

"Maybe he won't come," said Boomer. "It's a long way."

"He doesn't care," Tyler said. "He doesn't care how long it is."

"He don't know where you are, though, right?" Boomer asked.

"Not now," Tyler said. "But he'll look, and he'll ask. He'll tell people I'm his little sister. I don't know, something like that, and he's got to find me to tell me all is forgiven? He can get cleaned up and be real, you know, winning. He's in a war with Satan, and he'll do whatever it takes for as long as it takes."

"I don't get it about the war with Satan," Boomer said. "I

mean, I don't see what your part in that is. You ain't Satan. Or am I wrong?"

"No," said Tyler. "It's complicated. I'm kind of like a spy? You'll have to ask Hulon."

"That's okay," said Boomer. "No need to trouble him. I'll try to work it out for myself."

"What am I going to do?" Tyler asked. "Hugh says don't worry, he'll take care of him. But that's a joke. He doesn't know Hulon. He doesn't know what he is. He hasn't got any idea."

"No," Boomer said. "He don't."

"He couldn't stand against Hulon," Tyler said.

"He might try," Boomer said.

"He wouldn't last five minutes," Tyler said. "Anyway, he won't be here. He's leaving. He's going away himself as soon as he can."

Boomer laughed. "No, he ain't," he said.

"He's not?" Tyler said. "He says he is."

"Sure, he does," Boomer said. "He pisses and moans about it here, how stupid it is, how it's noplace. Boring. Not for him. Never. He's got big plans. He'll be out of here, any day. But you don't see him picking up and going, do you? No. You don't, and you won't. The thing is, this is a tough place to leave. Young guys like him complain, but they don't move. Then when they get older they quit complaining, that's all that happens. What they don't do is get out."

"You did," Tyler said.

"Yeah, but I came back," Boomer said.

"You came back, yes, but that was your choice. The point is, you left," Tyler said. "You got out. So it's not always like you say."

"Yeah, it is," said Boomer. "It always is. Look. Here I am, you know? Well, how would you know? It's complicated, like you said. You're the bride of Satan, and I'm complicated."

"We're both complicated," Tyler said.

"Still," Boomer said. "I'd keep moving if I were you. Don't stay in one place. Don't just wait for him. Keep moving around."

"How?" Tyler said. "Keep moving, how? My car's a wreck. I'm about broke."

"Well, broke," Boomer said. "As far as money, Cordie would spot you a hundred, I bet. I'm good for fifty. It's something."

"I don't want you to think I don't appreciate it," Tyler said. "I do. But how far am I going to get on one-fifty after I've had my car fixed?"

"You ought to go to Garrett, then," Boomer said. "Hit him right, he might help you out. I'm not kidding."

"Garrett, Garrett, Garrett," Tyler said. "I've never even seen him. He's going to pay to fix my car?"

"Why not?" said Boomer. "Garrett. Hell, get him when he's crazy enough, he might buy you a new one. Give you his. Both."

"Why?"

"He don't need a reason. I'm just saying: if you want money, that's where it's at. Around here that's where the money is. At Garrett's. Garrett's like the bank. You need money? Go to the bank."

"Maybe I will," said Tyler.

"I would," Boomer said. "I would. I have."

"You have?" Tyler asked. "You know him?"

"Sure," Boomer said. "Everybody does."

"Not me," said Tyler. "What's he like?"

Two skidders, a front-end loader, five or six men, one truck. The truck was backed up to the landing at the bottom of the hill where already ragged logs in a pile as high as a house had been made ready. The skidders and the choppers were up in the woods, invisible, but the noise of the skidders went up and down: *ummm, ummm, UMMM, UMMM, ummm, ummm*. Below, the grabber arm on the truck clanked and rattled. It swung back and forth from the log pile. And in the air over the whole tiny valley the racket of the saws seemed to come from everywhere, like the clamor of crows at dawn.

Mr. Benteen watched and listened from his spot on the hillside opposite. Condostas had been in there a week. You couldn't yet see open ground where the loggers worked, though open ground would show soon enough. Now, where they had cut, the woods remained, but they looked dull, they looked gone-off, because their green was no longer the green of living trees but of their waste: fallen tops and branches left as they lay, chaotically, the leaves and needles dead but not yet turned brown. In another week the hillside would look like a battlefield. By the end of July, when Terry was done, it would look like a desert. Then they would use the loader to shove the tops and the slash into piles. Then they would burn the piles.

A country in transition.

The truck was loaded now. The driver, a tiny forked figure, was clamping down the chains that held the mountain of logs on his truck. He climbed into the cab. Benteen heard the engine. What was it, a quarter of a mile, air line, from where he stood? Four hundred yards? A good man with a rifle could get that driver from here. It was a dream Mr. Benteen entertained. Well, not to shoot the driver. The driver was a plain, honest man like any other, doing his job. But to shoot out one of those enormous tires, say, or the gas tank.

In an hour that truck would be back. Terry's choppers, Terry's loader, would be ready for it with more logs. In two weeks, desert. That's how deserts come. God don't make deserts, we do.

Well, this side was safe. This side was his. Terry wouldn't cut here, ever.

Not ever?

This side of the Dead River branch, Benteen's side, his domain, was safe, and it was a big domain, no doubt about that. But he could see the dark water lapping against his foundations all around. He could hear the horns of his enemy without his walls all around. By day he could see their engines and by night he could see their fires. What good is a domain if it has an end?

Here they come.

This is no drill.

"What is that stuff?"

"Cologne."

"Cologne? Perfume for guys."

"No perfume. Shit, no. I don't wear perfume. What do you think? This is cologne. Drives women crazy, says so on the bottle. It makes them want to jump right on you."

"Does it?"

"Doesn't it?"

"Shut up. Get rid of it. Wash it off."

"Wait a minute. Are you telling me you want me to not use it?"

"Yes."

"Not, you don't care. Not, it makes no difference to you. But, please don't use it?"

"Yes."

"Well, all right. That's something. That's a sign. That's what I wanted to hear."

"It is?"

"You know, you've got a nice back here?"

"Thank you."

"That's a hell of a back. You want to stand up so I can see?"

"Okay?"

"It's kind of a triangle."

"Sure, it is. You never saw a girl's back before?"

"Yeah, I have. I guess."

"You're more interested in the other side, mostly. Is that it?"

"That's true, but that is an excellent back. You've got muscles there."

"Course, I got muscles. What did you think?"

"I don't know. You've got those little places there, on either side. There, them. What are those? I don't think I've got those."

"That's not my back."

"Close enough. You've got a long back. Just a hell of a back. You want to come down here now?"

"I don't know. You think I should?"

"Oh, yeah."

"You want me to?"

"I do."

"You do?"

"That's good."

"Do you always get what you want?"

"Every time."

"Goodness. You're a real cannonball, aren't you? Is it true

43

you got kicked out of that college for beating up a professor?"

"Not exactly."

"What, exactly?"

"He wasn't a professor, and I didn't beat him up."

"Why did they kick you out, then, if you didn't do anything?"

"I didn't say I didn't do anything. I said he wasn't a professor. He was a football coach. And I didn't beat him up. I gave him one shot."

"And you did that why?"

"Something he said."

"What?"

"I don't remember."

"Sure, you do. What did he say?"

"He called me a two-percenter."

"What's that?"

"I don't know."

"You don't? You don't know? Let me see if I've got this right. You lay this guy out, get yourself kicked out of college, nearly land in jail, because he calls you a name that you don't know what it means?"

"Looks that way. If I'd known what it meant I probably would have killed him."

"My goodness, you're a fierce boy."

"That's right."

"Just fierce. And always get what you want, too. Goodness."

"Sure."

"Do what you want, get what you want. Who you want. I bet you're a terror with the girls."

"You know I am."

"Good looking, too."

"That's right."

"Prettiest thing around, somebody said. But the only thing is, come to think of it, kind of a big fish in a little pond, you know? Not much competition for you around here, is there? A big pretty fish in a little pond. You reckon that's what a two-percenter is?"

"Don't forget what happened to the last fellow called me that."

"What did? I mean, did you knock him out?"

"Cold. Busted his jaw, too. Greatest day of my life."

"You are fierce, all right. I wonder how you'd do up against Hulon."

"You got Boomer pissing his pants over that guy. He's scared to death."

"He's right to be scared to death."

"Did he really kill a guy with a sledgehammer?"

"I saw him do it. This guy, Javier? He wouldn't get out of his car. He locked himself in his car? He owed Hulon money. Hulon got this big hammer, beat down his door, smashed out his windshield. Then he pulled him out. By then the head had busted off. The hammer head? Hulon beat him with the handle. He was dead, all right, when he got done."

"Wow."

"Another time I saw him about kill a man with a fence post. A big old corner post? Hulon just picked it up and swung it like a baseball bat. But the guy ran off, got away. You want to look out for Hulon."

"I'm not worried about him."

"You should be. You ought to be. Goodness, that stuff is awful."

"You told me."

"Hulon wears it. Wore it."

"You told me that, too. Forget Hulon, okay? Hulon is back in Texas playing with himself."

"Not for long."

"You'll never see him again. And if you do, you let me worry about him."

"Hulon's no football coach, you know."

45

"I eat guys like that for breakfast. I'm not worried about him."

"You don't understand about Hulon, do you? All I told you, you still don't understand. Hulon is not like you. He doesn't care what happens to him. He doesn't care what he does."

"So what? Anyway, I've got friends that can take care of him if it comes to that. Which it never will."

"What friends? You mean Marvin?"

"Not Marv. God, no."

"Boomer?"

"Not Boomer, either."

"Who, then? Who are you talking about?"

"Friends not around here but I can call them in. Nobody you know."

"What are you talking about?"

"People who can get things done."

"I hope there's a lot of them."

"Or, I'll tell you what. We'll let Mom take care of him."

"That might work."

"Look, all I meant was, don't think about Hulon. Think about me. Think about being here, right here, now. Think about me."

"What are you doing?"

"I don't know."

"You're going to sleep on me, aren't you?"

"No chance."

"That's good, because your mama will be here in half an hour. Less. She might wonder what we're doing."

"I think she could figure that out, don't you?"

"I mean wonder why you're here now."

"I'll tell her I hurt myself."

"You told her that before."

"I hurt myself again. You're nursing me."

"Is that what I'm doing?"

"That's right."

"Hey, open your eyes, boy. Don't you go to sleep on me, now. Hello?"

M̲r̲. Townsend Higginbotham Guest, the, ah, dealer (partial estates, specialty lots, private sales, very quiet, very discreet), sat in a corner booth of a dark little place in the basement of an old building in Brattleboro. He sat with a weak Scotch whisky and soda before him and waited.

Mr. Guest operated out of the Boston area. He came through this part of the country three or four times in the course of a year. He was a man of sixty, spare, mature, handsome, with a lofty nose, his hair and mustache gray, clipped. He wore an old tweed jacket, white shirt, and blue tartan tie. Altogether, he might have been a master at an Episcopal boys' school in the old days, and in fact for some years he had been exactly that. His St. Bart's days were long ago now, but Mr. Guest still had that easy, amused, old-fashioned way with the young. When Hugh came into the room and approached his booth, Mr. Guest held out his hand and said, "My boy."

"How are you doing?" asked Hugh. He sat down across from Mr. Guest.

"Well, well," said Mr. Guest. "Good of you to come down. Will you have something? Beer?"

"Sure."

"Something to eat? Have you lunched?"

"Lunched?" said Hugh. "Yeah, I've lunched. It's past one."

"So it is," said Mr. Guest. A waiter came and he ordered Hugh's beer.

"Anyway, I can't take the time," said Hugh. "I have to get back up there. We're haying."

"Are you? How is it you were able to get away?"

"The baler threw a belt," said Hugh. "The parts place is here so I had to come down."

"Lucky it happened this afternoon, when we were to meet," said Mr. Guest.

Hugh grinned at him.

"Not giving yourself any inconvenience, are you?" asked Mr. Guest. "Not swimming too far from the dock?"

The waiter brought Hugh's beer. He asked Mr. Guest if he needed another whisky. Mr. Guest shook his head and the waiter left them.

"No problem," said Hugh.

"Well, then," said Mr. Guest. "We talked about a governess cart."

"A what?"

"The little carriage," said Mr. Guest. "You remember. Two wheels. Blue, you said. Red trim. In a shed someplace."

"That's right," said Hugh. "It's made like a basket. What's that?"

"Willow work."

"Willow?" said Hugh. "Well, yeah, I mean, it's there. It's not so little, though."

"How little?"

"Well, you've got the poles. For hitching it up? With the poles it's, I guess, here to the bar."

"That's an awkward size, isn't it?" said Mr. Guest.

"Saw the suckers right off," said Hugh. "The poles. Saw them right off. Then you just stick it in the back and go."

Mr. Guest smiled. "I hardly think so," he said.

"Well, then," said Hugh. "You'll need a trailer or something."

"Where is the thing?" asked Mr. Guest. "Now, you say it's in a shed but not at the big place. Not at the place where all the other goods are."

"No," said Hugh. "It's at the Lower Farm, in the shed there. We call it the Lower Farm. It's a couple of miles away."

"Not on the main road at all?"

"No," said Hugh. "The road's dirt. You could rent a trailer."

"I hardly think so," said Mr. Guest. "I can't go driving around your back roads in a damned U-Haul. Here is what occurs to me, though. We have a friend who can. Young Terry might be of help. That is what occurs to me. Those big trucks of his."

"You mean a log truck?" Hugh asked.

"Well, well," said Mr. Guest. "It doesn't have to be entirely loaded with logs, always, does it?"

"I could talk to Terry," Hugh said. "It would take some work."

"If it's as you describe it, if it's very pretty," said Mr. Guest, "then it's worth whatever's required. It's kept up, is it? It's in good condition?"

"Oh, yeah," said Hugh. "He's got tarps all over it. Paint's fresh. He even has Marv grease it, shine up the brass. It's like new."

"Then it's worth some work, to me," said Mr. Guest.

"But is it worth it to me?" said Hugh.

"I could say a thousand dollars this time," said Mr. Guest.

"Wow," said Hugh. "I take care of Terry?"

"Not necessarily," said Mr. Guest. "Make whatever arrangement with Terry you like. We can talk about it."

"I'll talk to Terry," said Hugh. "I'll get back to you. Wow, you know? I'm thinking. If it's worth a thousand up here, what are you going to get for it down there?"

"My boy," said Mr. Guest.

"Come on," said Hugh. "Ten? Fifteen?"

"I hardly know, my boy," said Mr. Guest.

"You know fucking-A well," said Hugh. "But you don't say. It's fine. Forget it. I'll get your little cart for you. I was just curious. Like, where do you sell something like that, anyway?"

"Oh, it's already sold," said Mr. Guest.

Hugh finished his beer.

"They're waiting on me," he said.

"Yes," said Mr. Guest. "In the haylands. I worked on a hay crew for a couple of summers when I was a boy in Maine. God, that was a long time ago. Before the war."

"What war?" said Hugh.

"I don't think we had a baler," said Mr. Guest. "I'm sure we didn't. We made the loads loose. The mower was pulled by a horse, I think. It was good hard work."

"It still is," said Hugh. "It still is hard work, you know? It didn't stop being hard work when you got too old to do it. You're starting to sound like Garrett."

"Well, well," said Mr. Guest. "He and I are friends, in a manner of speaking, aren't we? Partners, in a manner of speaking? I feel quite close to Garrett Benteen. Indeed I do."

What's he like? I said. Garrett? What's Garrett like? I don't know. God's sake.

I heard he's crazy, she said.

Well, I told her, he's not. You heard wrong.

He's not. Garrett's not crazy. When he used to drink a lot,

then, maybe. Garrett's got his ups and downs, Lord knows. But he's not crazy. He's got more money than's good for him. But no, I told her, I won't say anything against Garrett. He's always been good to us, and a lot more than us. He's generous. There's Vergil Percy, out there, there's others, too, more than a lot of people know.

Boomer says he's crazy, she said.

Boomer, I said. Hah.

No, Garrett's not crazy, though if you ask me his father was. Well, he was. His father was in and out of, like, asylums. He was crazy. Garrett—the thing is, Garrett's always had his own way in everything, so he looks crazy. Having your own way—I mean all the time—and being crazy come to the same thing, about.

Then she asked: Has he got a wife?

A wife? I said. I laughed. What do you care? I said.

Has he? she said.

Got two or three of them, I said. She laughed.

He's had two or three, anyway. And then there were plenty of others he forgot to marry. He moved them in there, he moved them out. The fact is, I told her, Garrett don't have the greatest reputation. He got around. But no, he didn't. He didn't get around. That was the trouble. He married from away. One was clear from England. None of them could stand it up here, but they couldn't get him to leave so they took off. I don't think any of them lasted two years. The English one, Diana. She rode. You know? With the funny britches and the black coat and little helmet, like? Goodness, she was a sight. Beautiful woman. My husband used to call her the queen. She thought she was, too. She didn't last long, like I said.

So he's by himself? she asked.

Uh-oh, I thought.

You keep clear of him, lady, I told her. You got trouble enough without taking on Garrett. Not because he's not all right. I won't say anything against him. There's no mean streak to him, I'll say that. He's not crazy, either, but also he's not getting any less crazy, if you see what I mean. Garrett's got his ups and downs, like everybody else. Well, not like everybody else.

You like him yourself, don't you? she said. You do.

Althea, the housekeeper, was hanging Vergil's underwear on a line at the side of the house when Hugh drove into the lane with Mr. Benteen. Even in June Vergil wore his long underwear; he wore it all year round. Indeed, if it hadn't been for Althea, he'd have worn the same suit, never changed it. Vergil didn't care. He was past looking after himself. Althea was a cousin of his, a niece, some relation.

She had brought a chair from the house and was standing on it so she could hang the underwear out full length from the high line. She turned from the line to see who had driven up. Behind her three suits of underwear hung in a row by their long sleeves, stirring uneasily in the air like ghosts who are giving up, who are trying to say, *Don't shoot*.

Hugh stopped the car in front of Vergil's house, and Benteen opened his door.

"Come on," he said to Hugh.

"I'll wait out here," said Hugh.

"Come on."

"That's okay," said Hugh. "I'll just wait for you."

"No," said Benteen. "Come on."

Hugh opened his door and got out of the car. Althea had climbed down from her chair and come over. She held out a hand to Benteen.

"Well, well," said Althea. "That's your new car I heard about, I guess."

"That's it," Benteen said.

"Just look at that," said Althea. "Where would you get a car like that, now?"

"Out of Boston, this one," Benteen said.

"Out of Boston. What would a car like that cost?" said Althea.

"Couple of million," Benteen said. "Three."

"Think of that," said Althea. "And here's your driver, I guess."

"That's him," said Benteen.

Hugh thought Althea was crazy. She was always looking at you and she shook hands with you like a man and she talked like a man. Well, not like a man, but not like any other woman he knew. Althea was the size and shape of a fifty-five-gallon drum. She wore thick glasses that made her eyes bug, and altogether she looked like a frog—not a real frog but a frog made of crockery or plastic that you put in your garden.

"Go ahead in," said Althea. Mr. Benteen and Hugh followed her into the house by the side door, into the kitchen.

The kitchen was the room they lived in. It took up most of the rear of the house, a long room with west windows. It was dark in there and it smelled funny at first but it wasn't dirty. Also there was a lot of stuff. There were newspapers and magazines piled up, there were boxes and bottles and jars and tools. But it wasn't a mess; the stuff was neat.

The house had been Vergil's family's place, their farm. Vergil had worked it in his time, but not much. Mostly he'd worked at the mill in town or for Benteen or Benteen's father or Benteen's grandfather. When he'd got too sick to work he'd gone into the Soldiers' Home in White River, but a couple of years ago it looked like he didn't have much time left and he'd moved back here with Althea to take care of him. Now Vergil seemed as though he'd go on the way he was forever. He couldn't talk and he couldn't walk, but he knew who you were. Probably he did.

Vergil was sitting by the windows in a wooden wheelchair. He might have been asleep. A blanket covered his lap and legs and over his shoulders he wore a bright green jacket that said BOSTON CELTICS. Where had he gotten that? Who would give him that? People brought Vergil all kinds of clothes: hats and scarves and socks, even neckties, the way savages bring their rags and ribbons to hang on an ancient tree or to lay before a blank stone idol. No more than a tree or a stone did Vergil know or care what he wore. He didn't know, probably, what the Boston Celtics were. Didn't care.

Benteen went over to him and said hello. Vergil looked up at him and raised his hand. Benteen shook it. He brought a chair over.

"You're sitting in here by yourself," he said.

Hugh waited by the door. *Who's going to sit with him? McHale? Bird? Course he's by himself.*

Althea smiled at Hugh.

"You want some coffee?" she asked.

"Nothing," said Hugh.

"Soda?"

"Nothing," said Hugh. He stood by the door.

"I brought this boy," said Benteen. Vergil nodded to Hugh. Hugh nodded back. "I brought him to see you."

"Cordie Blankenship's boy," Althea said to Vergil.

"He's my driver," said Benteen. "He drove me out here today."

Vergil nodded, smiled a little. He kept his left hand under the blanket that covered his lap. Under there, Hugh knew, the old fellow was playing with his balls. You never saw that left hand, it was under the blanket—but the blanket moved. Hugh nodded to Vergil, smiled. Why does a dog lick his balls? Because he can. That kind of thing.

Benteen turned to Althea.

"How have you been?" he asked.

"Not too bad," said Althea. "Not too bad. His shoulder pains him some, I think. He don't complain. I took him for his checkup last week. That young man looked him over, told him he had the heart of an eighty-five-year-old. Was that meant to be a joke?"

"I expect it was," Benteen said.

"I didn't like it," said Althea. "I didn't like it and I didn't like him. I didn't say anything, though."

"Good," said Benteen.

Hugh watched them. Benteen stood in front of the window, looking down at Vergil. Althea waited by the sink. Vergil had forgotten them for the moment. He was looking out the window to the back lot and the woods enclosing it. The house was in the middle of the woods now.

Vergil wasn't a bad looking old party: had plenty of hair, all white; had the brown skin of someone who had worked outdoors, but not much lined, as though Vergil was so old he'd lost even his wrinkles; had maybe half his teeth; had blue eyes that came and went, turned darker and paler as Vergil's attention passed in and out behind them like an animal moving through woods.

"Have you got everything you need?" Benteen asked Althea.

"We need wood," said Althea. "We could use some wood."

"Wood?" Benteen said. "It's going to be July."

"He's cold all the time," said Althea.

"All right," said Benteen. "How much have you got?"

"Oh, a week, I guess."

"I'll get him to bring you some out," said Benteen. "We'll fill the dump truck."

Althea nodded.

Benteen pulled a stool beside Vergil's wheelchair and sat down. Vergil looked at him.

"What about those birds?" Benteen asked him. "How are those birds of yours? You had any new ones?"

"I should say so," Althea said. "Show him. Go on, show him."

With his right hand Vergil reached down beside him in the chair and brought up a paperbound book, *Birds of North America*. He laid it on his lap and went through it one-handed. His other hand stayed under the blanket at his crotch. Vergil's fingers turned from page to page through the book. His hand was enormous, Hugh saw.

Vergil spread the book open at a page of colorful birds. He pointed at one and looked at Benteen. Althea came behind them and looked over Vergil's shoulder.

"What's that one?" Benteen asked.

"That's a yellow-bill magpie," Althea said. She grinned at Benteen. "Just this morning, that one was here."

"Is that right?" Benteen said.

Vergil turned the pages and stopped at another plate. He pointed again at another bird. He was excited now. He stabbed his finger onto the page.

"By Jesus," said Benteen. "Look at that one."

"That be a swallow-tail kite," said Althea, leaning down to read the legend on the plate.

"I see it," said Benteen. "By Jesus."

The birds were imaginary—well, not imaginary; they lived, but not in Vergil's yard, except through the gaudy pictures in his book. That magpie is a California bird, the kite is from the Gulf of Mexico. There were a dozen others. Vergil pulled them out of the book and then saw them in his plain New England dooryard.

Althea and Marvin Bland, thinking to give Vergil something to look at while he sat at his window all day long, had put up a post just beyond the window and set on it a little railed platform for a bird feeder. They scattered seeds on it, corn, and waited for feathered friends to come and entertain Vergil. They came, too: chickadees and nuthatches, little gray birds.

Then Benteen on one of his visits had brought the book so Vergil and Althea could look up any birds they didn't know that might arrive. Immediately Vergil began to see them, to find them in *Birds of North America*. Vergil's birds were always the most exotic, gaily colored, boldly marked species. Parrots, flamingos, cuckoos, tropical humming-birds, Mexican finches—birds of the Pacific Coast, of the Rio Grande, of the Antilles, birds that never occurred north of Miami—these Vergil discovered in his book, then looked up and found at his own window.

"He likes the brighty ones," Althea said.

"That kite, there," said Benteen. "That's nothing but a fancy buzzard. You see too many of those coming around you, you got a problem."

Althea grinned and shook her head. "That's right," she said.

Vergil looked at Benteen. His finger rested on the picture of the exquisite kite.

"He saw that one last week," said Althea. "Then again just the other day."

"Well, I'll tell you," said Benteen. "Some of those parrots. You see one of them, you get your net and bring him right in here. Some of them are worth real money."

"I should say so," Althea said.

Vergil had forgotten the birds now. His hidden hand had stopped moving under the blanket while he showed them the picture of the kite, but now Hugh saw he was at it again down there. He let the book slip off his lap and fall to the floor. Benteen bent and picked it up, set it on the win-dowsill.

"Look," he said. "Look what I brought." He took a little

round can of snuff from his pocket. He opened it and showed it to Vergil. Vergil looked down at the snuff. He nodded. His hand stirred in his lap under the blanket.

Benteen laid the can of snuff in Vergil's lap. Vergil stuck his right thumb and forefinger into the can and took out a dip of the black, greasy tobacco. He brought it up to his mouth, but his hand shook. He spilled the snuff down his front. Vergil shook his head.

"Here," said Benteen.

Oh, shit. Oh, come on.

"I'll get it," said Benteen.

Slowly, gently, he reached for Vergil's mouth. With his left hand he took hold of Vergil's lower lip and drew it out a little, then picked up a dip of snuff with his right little finger and, not spilling any, tucked it carefully under Vergil's lip. Vergil nodded, his mouth worked. He looked out the windows. Benteen wiped his fingers on his pants. Hugh looked away.

Shit.

"That dirty stuff," said Althea. "At least he don't smoke. I wouldn't be here if he smoked."

"Neither would he," said Benteen. Althea laughed.

"Neither would he be here," Benteen said.

Althea turned to the sink and took an empty coffee can down from a shelf beside it.

"I'll get him to bring you a load," said Benteen. "Don't know just when, but I won't let you run out. You need anything else, call."

He stood up, laid a hand on Vergil's shoulder.

"We'll see you," Benteen said. "You see any good ones, you get that net, get them right in here for me. Will you do that?" Vergil looked up at him. A little rill of brown snuff juice was beginning to form at the corner of his mouth. Althea saw it and handed him the coffee can. Hugh went out the kitchen door with Benteen behind him.

They got into the Mercedes and Hugh started it up. He turned around in front of the house and drove out the lane. The lane at Vergil's was so grown up with brush that whips hit the car on either side as they drove out.

"I've got to cut some of this out," said Benteen. "It's like a jungle. When that old fellow was your age, I bet you could see clear from here to town. It was all farmland, cleared land. Now it's a jungle. He must hate that. The poor old bastard."

"What's he poor for?" Hugh said. "He sits there all day long with nothing to do, she takes care of him. He don't have to do anything but bounce his balls around, dawn to dark. Don't sound too rough to me."

"The thing is about those birds," Benteen said. "None of them is really here. None of them ever comes around here. He just thinks he sees them because they're in the book."

"Fucking gaga," Hugh said.

"You'd call it that," Benteen said. "You know who the president was when he was born?"

"George Washington."

"I don't, either," said Benteen. "But it had to been, say, Cleveland, McKinley, them. Do you know who the president was when you were born?"

"No," said Hugh. "What do I give a shit?"

"Me, was old Cal Coolidge," said Benteen. "Came from right over the mountain, here. Good old Cal. President for six years. Didn't do a god damned thing. Those were the days. Nixon. You were Nixon. Tricky Dick. I voted for him, but only once."

"I wouldn't vote for any of them," said Hugh. "They ought to all be shot."

"Easy to say," said Benteen. "Who's going to shoot them? You? That old guy I'm pretty sure would have to be Cleveland. He was in World War I, a soldier. I bet he never went anywhere farther than Brattleboro, White River, any other time in his life, but he went to France. He came home and never moved again, but he went clear to France in 1917."

"Must be that's where he learned to jerk off," said Hugh.

"Tomorrow," said Benteen. "You and Marv, you load the dump truck, get it all loaded. Then next day, I mean first thing, you take it out there and see it's all got in for her, all put up for them out there."

"Tomorrow," said Hugh.

"What's he like? Garrett? What do you care?"

"Boomer says I should ask him for money to get my car fixed."

"Why would he do that?"

"Boomer says he's crazy."

"He's harmless."

"Not like you, you mean?"

"Me? No, I'm harmless, too. I can show you how harmless I am."

"You just showed me. What do you do for him, anyway?"

"For Garrett? More than he knows."

"What does that mean?"

"Nothing. Oh, you know, I do a little of this, a little of that. Hump hay, dig holes."

"And drive. You drive that big car for him."

"That, too."

"Boomer says he's rich."

"Garrett ain't that rich. He owns land."

"How much land?"

"A lot. I don't know."

"What are you doing?"

"Nothing."

"Listen. Wait. How much land?"

"I told you. I don't know. A lot. If it's around here, Garrett probably owns it. Garrett don't like to not own things. Can we stop talking about him now?"

"Boy."

"What?"

"I'm thinking."

"Don't. Don't think. See? That's better. That's so much better."

"Wait. I said, wait a minute."

"Why? What?"

"So, what's he like?"

PART II

The deputy had a flashlight, a black thing not less than a couple of feet long. He used it to push open the door of the shed. He looked into the shed. Mr. Benteen followed him, but the deputy turned and said, "You want to wait out here?"

"Why?" Benteen said. "Nobody's there. There's nothing to see."

"It's a crime scene," the deputy said. "I don't want it contaminated until we check it out."

"Contaminated?" said Benteen. "What are you talking about? This is my place. There's nothing here."

"I'm telling you what the procedure is," said the deputy. "This is a crime scene."

"Well, god damn it to hell," said Benteen.

The deputy went into the shed alone. He switched on his light. He didn't walk around much but moved the light over the floor, into the corners, up into the rafters. Under the roof beam there were two or three bats hanging, and when the light reached them they shifted and squeaked.

"You got bats in here," the deputy called out.

The floor of the shed was rough wood planks. Straw was spread over them, and some of it had been kicked up, but there were no tracks. The deputy left the shed.

"Well, you got a floor to it in there," he said to Benteen. "There ain't a lot to see."

"That's what I told you," said Benteen.

The shed had double doors that swung out. They had nothing to hold them shut but an iron hasp and a bent spike. Now they stood open. They were flimsy doors.

"No lock on this?" the deputy asked.

"No," said Benteen.

"You made it easy for him, didn't you?" the deputy said.

Benteen didn't answer him.

"Well, I'll look around," said the deputy. "Go see Terry. See what Terry's got to say. It won't do any good."

"Terry again," said Benteen.

"Terry was here," said the deputy. "This is Terry. He took your cart. You want to know what he did? I'll tell you: he put it on one of his trucks, threw a tarp over it, hid it some way, I don't know, and drove it away. Sure, he did. Here, you can see the tracks the logger left right here. See that tread? That's Terry."

"Go get it back, then," said Benteen.

"Well, I'll go see him," the deputy said. "But I don't know. Terry's cute. Unless I find him with it, moving it, well, he's cute. He's hooked up to some big thief down country. We've been watching him for months."

"We?" Benteen said. "You and who?"

"Well," the deputy said, "you know: me, some others."

"All right," said Benteen. "You told me the last time."

The deputy shut the doors of the shed. He closed the rusty strap that held them and looked for the spike that secured the strap, but it was missing. When the deputy left the doors, they swung slowly open again.

"You ought to get a real door on here that you can put a real lock to," he said.

"This shed has never had a lock." Benteen said.

"That's what I'm telling you," the deputy said. "Time was, this was all you'd need, you wouldn't even have a lock to it. Time was. Now you got to have real doors, real locks. This way you make it easy for him."

"No locks," Benteen said.

The deputy shook his head.

"Suit yourself," he said. "It's your place. I'm telling you, though. I'm telling you, that's all."

The shed sat no more than seven or eight feet from the road. The deputy walked from the door to the road. He turned to Benteen.

"You make it easy for him," he said. "All he does, he drives right up, goes in, rolls the thing out of there, gets it up on his truck, drives away."

"It's not small," Benteen said. "It must be eight, nine feet long, weigh a hundred pounds."

"Well, sure," the deputy said. "He had to had some help. No question he had some help. Question is, Who? Who helped him?"

I brought this boy.

I brought him to see you.

Cordelia's boy.

My driver.

Well, fuck you.

Like he was introducing me to the president, to somebody a little bit important, instead of that old bastard sitting out there cranking his wank. Jesus. He never let it alone. I thought I was bad. Vergil's must be getting ready to fall off. Must be he's got to keep it in shape for that Althea. There's a number, holy Christ. You think about it, how many women are there who you would *not* take on? Even waifs. I mean if you had the chance, if there was no trouble to it, if everything was right, if everything was easy? How many are there you'd flat refuse? Not many. But Althea? Sorry, Althea, can't do it. Sorry, good-bye, got to run.

Still, she lights up old Verg's board, I guess. Suppose they're into it out there? At his age? At hers? Looking like he does? Like she does? They say there's no reason you can't keep right at it, all the way to the end of the line. Maybe not as much, but what the hell? And it's not like there's a lot else to do out there: no TV. So why not? Get her some fancy nightgowns, something black? Or, no: that oil, get some of that oil you put on all over you, some of that musk. Now you're talking. Get that Althea all wound up, I God, she'll purr like a kitten.

Course the neighbors are not going to like it, even though there aren't any neighbors. They are going to disapprove all to hell and gone. Carrying on like man and wife. At his age. At hers.

Give it to him, though. Give Verg some credit: he don't give a shit. He's sitting there day in, day out, cranking away, drooling away, nodding away, seeing birds from I don't know, fucking Africa. Don't know where he is, don't care. The whole town can come out there and look in the window. The whole town can disapprove all it wants to. He wouldn't stop. He wouldn't do one thing different. He wouldn't care. Give him that.

Garrett, the same. What's Garrett get out there? I brought this boy. My driver. Thanks a lot. He goes out there like he was going to church, like Vergil'd saved his life, like he owed Vergil money instead of the other way around. What's he get? He waits on him. He's all over How have you been? What do you need? He sticks Vergil's fucking chaw down for him—Christ, I liked to puke.

He's pretending, Garrett is. He's playing at them. Lord of the manor, but good, you know? A regular guy. Generous. He's pretending at them, and he's bringing them in. He wants everybody to know what a great guy he is even though they also know he's a stupid, rich, crazy, fuck-up drunk. They'll say, How bad can he be? How bad can he be?

They'll say, Look: he pulled old Vergil Percy out of the Soldiers' Home, free for nothing, bought his place, brought him home, fixed it up, set Vergil up out there with all expenses paid and his own sixty-five-year-old, live-in frog-face female. What a guy, right? He brings them into his thing that way. They get, like, a place to live, a job, help. He gets to go on with his thing.

Not bad, not bad at all. Was me, now, though, I believe I'd go ahead and trade Althea in on a TV. Otherwise, I got to say old Vergil didn't make a shabby deal at all.

D o I like him? Do I like Garrett? She would come out with something like that and you'd have to think. Garrett. Do I like Garrett? But of course the thing is—and here's where she's off base, because she's not from around here—it don't matter. I don't have to like him or not like him. I said I did, though.

I do, I said. Course I do. All the things he's done for people around here. Course I like him. Vergil Percy, for one. Vergil'd been dead years ago if Garrett hadn't bailed him out.

I don't know him, she said.

And you won't, I said. Vergil lives way out of town and he don't go out. He'd old. I mean really old. Garrett treats Vergil like some kind of hero. I never understood why. All he really is is a dirty old man who's too old to get in trouble any more. Vergil's no prize.

What do you mean bailed him out? she said. Was he in jail?

No. I don't mean that way, I said.

Vergil was old. He was sick, couldn't work. He never had any money. He was living in the Soldiers' Home in White River. That's nothing but a dying house up there, even though half the people there were never really soldiers, fighting soldiers, although Vergil was. Give him that. He was in World War I, went to France. So did my granddad, though, and nobody ever made a fuss over him—well, but then he died younger. Garrett got Vergil out of there, bought up Vergil's old place out there toward Dead River Settlement. House and fifty acres. Vergil hadn't lived there for probably thirty years, but Garrett figured he'd bring him home to spend his last weeks at the old place. You know. He set Vergil up out there with that Althea Fallowfield to look after him. She's his niece, grandniece, I don't know. That one's a piece of work, too, Althea. She and I are some kind of cousins. Not but what she don't take good care of Vergil. But if you say she takes such good care of Vergil, I have to say she's well paid for it. By Garrett. Not but what she isn't a good person, like everybody says. Althea's so good, they say. You heard of too good? That's what I mean by bailed him out. Garrett saved his life, made him a place. Took on a little more than he was looking for with it, too.

That made me laugh to think. Garrett thought he was buying a, I don't know, a pair of pants. It turned out he was buying the whole store.

I told her.

When Garrett moved Vergil out there, it was spring, early summer—around this time. Nobody thought Vergil'd last more than a couple of weeks. Now, that house was a wreck. Nobody had been living there, you see, it had stood empty and it was in tough shape. Garrett had it cleaned up, fixed the windows, but that was all he did because he didn't figure Vergil for more than a couple of weeks out there. Well, got to be fall, got cold. So Garrett had to have the chimney fixed so they could get some heat. Got to be November, December. Garrett had to have the roof fixed, it leaked. Had to have the electric run out there. Telephone. They hadn't any of that, and now Garrett had to have them hooked up out there.

Then in the spring Vergil perked right up, looked smarter than he had in years, started going in to the clinic. So Garrett had to buy them a car so Althea could get him down there. Garrett, I guess, takes a look, thinks, Boy, I got twenty, thirty thousand dollars in this thing. This was supposed to be an easy one. That was six years ago. Vergil's going strong, he's going to live forever. Send the bill to Garrett.

I said to Garrett one time, talking about Vergil, Well, it looks like you took on a little more than you bargained for out there. He just smiled. So I said, You going to take care of me when I get old? And he said, That smart mouth you got on you, we'll never know.

You said that woman was his niece, what's her name? she asked me.

Althea, I said.

Althea. She's his niece?

That's right. Niece, grandniece.

And she's your cousin?

That's right.

So that means you're some relation of Vergil's, too, she said.

I suppose so, I said. I suppose you could prove I was. I don't much brag about it, though.

Are you related to Benteen? she asked me.

That, I said, I am not.

I am not, though in a way she's right. Well, she's not right, because that's not what she said, but about me liking him or not. It don't matter. And in that way it's like we were family, Garrett and me. More than me, too. Others he's done things for, helped: more than most people know. Not just Vergil and not just us, paying his way to Hanover. Tommy, the one they call Boomer: Garrett took him on, and he was no prize, Boomer, whatever his mother may think. The inn, too, for that matter. It wouldn't be here. Garrett's given people jobs, paid their debts, paid them wages. Helped them. He's helped people who won't take help. He's done a lot, Garrett, more than most know about.

But then, Daddy, if you were to say all that when he was around or somebody else would, talking about Garrett like that, his generosity, Daddy would look at you and kind of raise one eyebrow and say, Does Job fear God for nought?

Marvin was saying they weren't from around here. They came down from the north, from Maine, from Canada. Big. He had sat there and watched it. Big, is right: the size of a horse. Horns like tree branches and the thing itself the size of a horse and not a little horse. Six feet at the shoulder, he said, more than that.

"Come on," said Hugh.

"Oh, sure," said Marvin. "At the shoulder he's taller than me. Just a hell of a thing. You think it's like a deer. This is no deer. You don't see them much. They come down from up north."

"Why?" said Hugh.

"I don't know," said Marvin. "They're passing through, I guess, on their way to someplace."

"Probably New York," said Hugh. "Looking for some-place they can have a little fun. That ain't here. You ready?"

"Ready," said Marvin.

They were making the hayload. Marvin was up top and Hugh was throwing. He bent, took hold of one of the square bales lying on the ground, and in one rising motion stood, brought the bale up to the height of his head, and tossed it lightly to Marvin atop the loaded bales stacked in the wagon. When they were done the load would be as high as a second-story window. No doubt it was because Hugh could throw a bale of hay ten feet into the air and keep on doing it all day long that the footballers at Dartmouth had believed he might be serviceable. They had their reward. Was pitching hay the highest and best use of Hugh, after all?

"When I was a kid there was one of them came into town," Marvin said. "It came right down the street, down one side, turned around, went back up the other side. Everybody saw it, followed it. It stopped at the school. That was the old schoolhouse, there, had a little fence out front. It went through the gate and it stood in the yard, and there it stayed. Well, of course those kids—one of them was me, I guess. That school just emptied out: *Look. Look at that*, you know. It just emptied right out. Nobody knew what to do, and they were afraid somebody would get hurt. They were afraid it would spook, you see, and somebody would get hurt. It wouldn't go away. Everybody was in the street, in the schoolyard, kind of keeping back from it, hanging back, it just standing there. Kids larking all around. Nobody knew what to do.

"And then Valentine, he was constable then, was there, and he kept a revolver in his car. He wasn't going to shoot it, but he thought he'd scare it off. So he fired into the air. The thing just looked at him. He fired again. It didn't move. So Valentine was for going out to Benteens' because it would have been Garrett's father then had a big-game rifle, like an elephant gun, and Valentine said he was through fooling with it. It would not go away. But then Mrs. Mackenzie came through the crowd, there, and went right up to it and stamped her foot and said, *Git*. And the thing shied around like a horse, it turned, and took off around the schoolhouse, around back. It was trotting, kind of, moving pretty good. It took the whole back fence down and then it was in the brook field and then it was over the brook and in the woods and gone. Mrs. Mackenzie said *Git* and it got. Her about ninety years old and four and a half feet high. About up to its knee. *Git*, she said. That was quite a thing, at the time. That moose."

"Yeah," said Hugh. "A moose in the street. It don't get much better than that. Not around here. Ready?"

"Ready," said Marvin.

Marvin caught the bale Hugh tossed up and set it in its place on the load. He built the load carefully, thoughtfully, the way you build a brick wall—a brick wall without mortar. There was art to the laying in of the bales so the load would mount to its full height and still remain stable of its own weight, even when it was rolling down from the field over the bumpy woods track. A good man could build a load of bales a mile up, if a thrower could be found to toss that high.

Sometimes they used two-by-four stickers run into the load to distribute its weight. Then you could build higher still. Then, also, you could leave a cavity inside the load, a hole, a room. That was a useful trick. More than a little liquor, for instance, moved through Vermont in a load of baled hay in the bad old good old days, and there is no reason why the same device, well known to traditional haymakers, or a like one, can't serve for certain private cargos, even today.

"It was with a bunch of deer," Marvin said. "It'd better look out. People find out it's here, they'll be after it."

"You?"

"Maybe," said Marvin. "Course, a big guy like him, you've got to think it through. This is no deer. You get your deer, you know, you dress him and drag him out. This thing probably weights half a ton. You've got him down out there, way off the road. What are you going to do with him?"

"Leave him out there," said Hugh. "So what?"

"You oughtn't to do that," said Marvin. "And then, of course, you're not supposed to shoot them in the first place."

"Course not," said Hugh. "But fuck it, right? What else are you going to do with them? That's the idea, right? Ready?"

"Ready."

They were well into the load by now, and it went up almost without effort from either of them. Hugh hardly had to lift the bales; maybe that is what Dartmouth didn't understand. He hardly lifted them, hardly threw them. Marvin hardly caught them. The bales were weightless by now. The air took their weight. They rose up from the field like trout from a brook, they hung in the air, they settled down into place on the load, feathers dropping onto the still surface of a pool, so softly, so easily that way.

"Is that him?" Tyler asked.

"Which?" Boomer said.

"In the corner, looking out."

"That's Garrett," said Boomer. "That's his spot."

"That's Mr. Benteen?" said Tyler. "He doesn't look like much, does he? I thought he was the man that came to cut the grass."

"Yeah," said Boomer. "Well, Garrett isn't much of a dresser, I guess."

"Not much of a dresser?" said Tyler. "He looks like an old drunk, he's been sitting there for two hours. Doesn't he ever have anything to eat?"

"Sometimes he does, sometimes he doesn't," Boomer said. "He's waiting for Hugh to come drive him home."

"I don't get that at all," said Tyler. "Why doesn't he drive himself? He's got that fancy car."

"I don't know," Boomer said. "He likes to get driven. I think his license was taken away."

"He's old," Tyler said.

"Yeah," said Boomer. "Well, older than you, anyway. Older than me. He doesn't approve of my hair."

"Well," Tyler said. "I don't see why he can't look nice when he comes in. If he's so rich why can't he get cleaned up a little?"

"Maybe you better ask him that," Boomer said.

"Maybe I will," Tyler said.

"You can be straight with Garrett," Boomer said. "Give him that: There's no bullshit to him."

"Still," Tyler said. "He doesn't have to look like a derelict. Look at him. Mrs. Blankenship wouldn't let most people in the dining room looking like that."

"You got that right," said Boomer. "But then, she can't really keep him out, can she?"

"She can't?" Tyler said. "Why can't she? I would. Looking like that. Like an old derelict."

"I mean, it's his place."

"What?"

"It's his place," said Boomer. "He owns it, Garrett does. This place, you know? It belongs to him."

"It does?" Tyler said. "He owns this too? Goodness. What is there around here he doesn't own?"

"Not a lot," said Boomer.

Does Job fear God for nought? Daddy would say. What he meant was, if Garrett's real generous, well, he's got a real lot to be generous with.

Benteens have always had it. It seems as though Garrett's father, or grandfather, it was, made a lot of money out west years ago. Mining or it might even have been oil he was into, oh, a long time ago. But even before him they were here and they were big. Land. They bought up farmsteads, timber. Somebody said Garrett's place here in town, all of it, is the biggest farm holding on this side of the state. He goes clear from here out to Dead River and then down the other way over the town line. And then up. Must be several thousand acres. Then there's the buildings, must be it's three separate farms, joined up, no four, and all the barns and so on. Marvin's place. The places in town. The inn. Garrett has a lot of real estate.

Now, what that might mean in cash money I don't know. He bought that car, I know that. He was ready to buy that whole mountain from Condostas only they wouldn't sell. But what would it come to, really? Not counting the buildings. Suppose Garrett's got, suppose, five thousand acres. Suppose he's got ten. Suppose land today costs, averaging, oh, thousand dollars an acre.

My, my.

Well, I know: there are ballplayers and movie people, there are eighteen-year-olds making that much in a year today. But still it ain't too bad for a fellow who just sits up here in the hills and farms. Sort of farms. And I didn't count the buildings.

Course it's not worth nothing 'til you sell it.

Across the green from the inn was the village church, white, its steeple lost in the trees except at the top where it rose above them. Mr. Benteen's table in the dining room let him look across to the church. There were lights in the what do you call it, the vestry, and six or eight cars were parked out front. AA had its meetings there. Having an AA meeting in that town without Benteen was like having Easter at St. Peter's without the Pope, but they'd have to get on without him the best way they could.

The church dated from 1825. It looked the way they all do: a long box, a tower, a pointed steeple. It might have been built by a child with his blocks—it had that rigor, it had that perfection. The perfection was real, but was the church?

Ten years earlier the vestrymen had solicited bids for replacing the old clapboard siding of the church building with vinyl panels imitating clapboards. There had been a hell of an uproar in the town. People who had never entered the church, Mohammedans, Zoroastrians, Hindoos, Democrats, had expressed outrage that a historic building, an authentic, pristine treasure of New England village architecture, was to be despoiled by fake clapboards—in effect, by plastic.

A meeting was held. The vestry's committee on siding took the position that vinyl clapboards were cheaper than wood, you didn't have to paint them, and they lasted forever.

The Mohammedans, Zoroastrians, Hindoos, and Democrats didn't care. The church was perfect, they said, it was immaculate. Vinyl siding would, quite simply, destroy it.

It looks just like wood, the committee on siding said. You can't tell the difference.

Of course you can, said the Mohammedans and others. It's plastic. It's the difference between a cheeseburger and filet mignon.

It's cheap, the vestrymen said. It don't need paint, it don't wear out.

To put vinyl siding on the Ambrose Church, the Mohammedans said, was nothing other than an act of vandalism.

About that point in the meeting, one of the siding contractors who was looking to submit a bid rose to observe that the vestry's published specifications referred only to installing siding on the body of the church building.

Aren't you going to cover the steeple? he asked.

Not at this time, said the committee on siding.

Why not?

We put vinyl up there fifteen years ago, the vestryman said.

* * *

The whole place was like that, the whole village, the whole town: it's what it was and it's what the thing it was has become. A matter of fifty houses, as the poet says. Closer to forty. Three country roads made a K, a little green in the middle, the village going out the four ways, first by house lots and front yards, then by bigger lots, given-over pastures, until you passed the last houses belonging to the village and were in the country again.

At the center of the village the green was a half-acre triangle with the church on one side and the inn obliquely opposite. Both structures today were entered on the lists of historic New England buildings, but they weren't the only places in the village to be distinguished that way. In 1939 or '40, at a time when the inn was in a state of neglect and disrepair and the town was without facilities for motorists, the Texaco company had moved to buy the inn from its then owner, with the purpose of tearing it down and putting in a filling station. After six months of quiet negotiations, Texaco had proposed a sales agreement to Mrs. Nightingale, widow of the innkeeper, and she had about decided to accept it. It was then that Benteen's father had learned of the plan. He went to Mrs. Nightingale and in an afternoon bought the inn for cash at Texaco's offer plus fifty percent. Texaco had been obliged to buy an open acre on the edge of the village for their station, which was built in the summer of 1941, the last summer before the war.

What war?

Here they come. This is no drill.

Today the Texaco station was the village's third historic building, having recently been added to the list on the recommendation of a panel of scholars and historians whose charge it was to enlarge the meaning of historic architecture beyond the usual churches, public buildings, and homes of the fortunate to embrace humbler structures. Thanks to them and to Benteen's father, therefore, the village had three undoubted monuments: classic church, classic inn, classic gas station.

All of it was true and all of it was of necessity

A country in transition, transition, transition.

Yes, it's like I said to old Marv: Hey, what else are you going to do with it, I said, you might as well blow it up. We're hunters up here, you know: if you can't milk it, or fuck it, or sell it to the tourists, you might as well shoot it. We're deer hunters up here, you betcha. Come November we'll gear up: five, six cases of beer, box of shells, couple of rolls of toilet paper, twenty-five pounds of doughnuts, the old thirty-thirty. When you get down to it, that's all a man really needs, right? Sit out there with your thumb up your ass for two weeks waiting for the brush to move.

Imagine if that was your life. Imagine if you thought that was fun. These guys are so fucking bored they think that's the best it gets from one year to the next. That big guy out there might as well walk in front of a train. If I was him and it comes November, I'd rather be anyplace else, anyplace: Beirut, Belfast, anyplace, come on, where's my ticket? Well, I would anyway. I've been deer hunting, too, you know. Fuck, yeah. Every couple of hours you let off a few just to keep awake.

Course Garrett might not like them going after that big guy. He might tell them they can't. Garrett figures he owns the land, he owns the woods, he owns the deer, and he owns that guy too as long as he's around. Garrett's the king. The old kings didn't just own the land, the country, right? They owned the deer, too. They even owned the people. Garrett likes that. Garrett could go for a piece of that action. He could. But those old kings are fucking gone, right? You know what happened to them.

How can you not go after somebody like that? Somebody that stupid, that crazy, that, you know, high? How can you leave him alone? Garrett thinks everything just sails along like it always has, him up on deck in the sun with a cool drink, everybody else down in the hold busting his ass—but happy down there, contented, loving it. How, if you're down in the engine room, do you not itch to wreck the whole thing, turn it upside down? Marvin? How do you do it, Marv? How do you play it straight?

Well, Marv's a patient man. And Marv's signed on for the whole voyage, hasn't he? Signed on for the whole fucking trip, right here. Not me.

Here they come, this is no drill, Garrett said. The evening I brought her over. He was sitting at his table after his supper and looking out the window. He didn't see me but when I came over he said, This is no drill.

Are you talking to me? I asked him

No.

Then you're talking to yourself, I said.

What did they do over there, after all? Garrett asked. Do you remember? With the church? Remember that flap a couple of years ago about whether to put vinyl siding up and nobody wanted to until it turned out the steeple already had it? Remember that?

Course I remember it. Foolishness.

And Walter told them, he said, Well, we put plastic on the steeple in 1970. It's been plastic up there for fifteen years. Did they go ahead and cover the rest of it then? Garrett asked.

I believe they stayed with boards, I said.

Garrett nodded.

Did you like your supper? I asked him, and he said, Sure,

and then I said, I don't know if you met my new girl yet, and I turned toward the kitchen door to see if she was where I could beckon her over, and there she was right behind me.

Tyler McClellan, I said, and Garrett got up and took her hand. Then he sat back down and looked at her.

You're the one running from the fellow in Texas that handles rattlesnakes, aren't you? Garrett said. Why does he do that?

And she said, Well, it's in the Bible.

Lot of things in there, Garrett said.

Hulon, that's my boyfriend, she said, he's fighting Satan.

Satan? Garrett said. You're from Texas. Where in Texas? he asked her. And she said someplace around Fort Worth.

I was in Texas, Garrett said. West Texas. Staked Plains. You ever been out there?

No, she said.

I didn't know you were out there, I said to Garrett. When was that? You were never out there.

Years ago, Garrett said. You don't know everyplace I been.

Glad of it, too, I said.

There's not a god damned thing out there, Garrett said. But rattlesnakes. Rattlesnakes they got. Used to see them in the road. Biggest god damned snakes I ever saw. Is that the kind?

Texas rattlers, is what Hulon calls them, she said. They're pretty big, I guess.

He must be nuts, Garrett said. Boys used to run over them in trucks on the road, it was like a sport. It felt like you ran over a log. One time I was driving along in a pickup with a bunch of Mexicans in the back and a kid driving, he saw one up ahead, almost across the road, cut over there, hit it, and when the back wheels went over it they pitched the snake up in the air behind and it landed in the back with the Mexicans. They all bailed out, eighty miles an hour we were going, they all jumped off right there. Mexicans and snakes all over the god damned road. You can have Texas.

Hulon comes from Arkansas, originally, she said.

You can have that, too, Garrett said.

When was he ever in Texas?

What are you doing up here? Garrett asked her.

Working, she said. Working for Mrs. Blankenship.

Working, Garrett said. He kind of just sat there and looked at her. How do you happen to be working here? he asked her.

I was on my way to Canada, she said.

Why? Garrett asked.

Get away, she said. Get away from my boyfriend. He's in jail at home, I didn't want to be there when he gets out. Would you?

You made it, Garrett said. You don't need to go clear to Canada. You're all right here. I hear you're screwing Cordie's boy.

God's sake, Garrett, I said. But I didn't need to have, for she spoke right up to him.

I don't know if that's your business, she said.

It ain't, Garrett said. Do you think one or the other of you women could bring me a cup of coffee and a small brandy, no more than an inch?

Then later she was all bent out of shape. She don't like the way he talked to her, questioned her. Who did he think he was? He didn't look to her like he was anything but an old bum. The way he dresses, the way he doesn't shave, the way he sits there at his table not talking to anybody, the way he's got no manners, none at all, the way he has a drink after supper. He's nothing but an old drunk, she said.

Wait a minute, I said. A lot of people have a brandy after supper. That don't make him a drunk.

It sure does, she said. Anybody who gets into it after supper is a drunk.

84

She don't miss much, I'll give her that. Garrett's cut down a lot, though he's not about to ever really quit. He was bad enough with it, I'll say that. He'd come in here with whatever wife or girl he had with him at the time out at his place, and the both of them would get just outrageous. Arguments. Well, fights. Brawls. I can show you a place on the bar where one of Garrett's girls picked up the fireplace poker one night and took a swing at him and missed, left a place it must be an inch deep in the wood. That's a mahogany bartop, you can't fix something like that. Now Tommy tells the guests that dent was made by an English soldier's sword, but the truth is it was some girl with a lot of liquor in her, who was probably no better than I won't say it—a slut—trying to brain Garrett.

Then there was the girl who bet Garrett he couldn't drive his truck up the steps and into the lobby and he said, Sure he could. He did, too. He drove right into the lobby, through the bar, through the dining room, and out the rear door. Almost. We had to close for a week. After that one, Homer Patch was the constable, he told Garrett if he ever caught him driving a car again, drunk or sober, it didn't matter, he'd have him locked up.

So, she's all bent out of shape. The same thing: she won't be talked to like that. And finally I said, Listen, I said, what's your problem? What do you expect? That's Garrett, you know? He's plain spoken. That's him. Take him or leave him. He's never going to jump up in your lap and lick your face. He ain't that kind of dog.

You ought to get a real door, here, that deputy had said, get a door you can lock. Good advice. Good advice: now that there's nothing much left to steal, we'll lock it up, nail it down. Why? When we had the treasure we didn't need a lock, now we've got the lock we've about lost the treasure.

This is no drill.

Mr. Benteen sat on a rock and looked across the little intervale to the near side of Judgment Hill, where Condostas were working. He no longer needed his glasses to see their progress. They had a third skidder working now. They were cutting pines. You could hear the trees going down. You could hear the chainsaw stop, then hear the tree start to crack, start to tear, hear the cracking go on and on, then the terrible thrashing, shuddering thump of the fall. The end of a world. By some trick of the wind today he could smell the sap of the cut pines, that beautiful smell.

Today it was plain they were doing a little more over there than cutting logs. Halfway up the cleared area a backhoe was working. They were digging a cellar hole. Condostas must be putting up a spec house. That would be the younger generation at work. Marco wouldn't fool with a house. He was a logger. He knew what he did. He was happy to cut and get out. It wouldn't occur to Marco to throw up an instant slum here by way of extracting the last possible buck from his ancient investment in that hillside. It's Terry's thing, Marco had said. Terry was the boy for that work.

The house would be lovely, Benteen knew, the architectural equivalent of a pimple. It isn't easy to make a fresh clearcut uglier than it is, but the house Terry was building would do it. It would be white. It would have a picture window. It would have either columns in front or fake brick half-siding or both. Terry would put it on the market for eighty thousand dollars, close for seventy. Five years later the house would begin to come apart at the seams like a cardboard carton left out in the rain. There would be other problems. In particular, on that site, which rose steeply in ledges from the valley bottom, you could save a lot of money by suggesting to the buyer that he simply piss off the front porch directly into the brook below; no need to run the stuff through an expensive septic system. Somebody would have to deal with that issue someday, but it wouldn't be Terry. He'd be long gone.

In no town in Vermont are there more than twenty-five sites where it's possible to build a house, and all of them are taken and have been for two hundred years. But people have to live someplace so they build in spots where houses are impossible, as here on Judgment Hill. All they build is trouble.

Mr. Benteen had an idea about housing in Vermont. He had a solution. You freeze the price of real estate at the level of, say, 1960. That will stimulate the hell out of the market and make everybody happy. But at the same stroke you prohibit new construction absolutely: everybody has to buy, sell, and occupy existing houses. In effect, you can swop or you can leave. Benteen called his measure the Woodpecker Policy, thinking of the way those useful birds nest in holes in trees, of which there is at any one time a fixed number, meaning that they must move, when they move, into holes formerly occupied by other woodpeckers. Benteen believed the Woodpecker Policy could work. It could save that country, but he knew it never would. It got you into politics, and in politics what works is what you can't do.

Terry was over there. That was Terry in the denim jacket and the cowboy hat. He was standing in the bed of a pickup truck watching the backhoe. The door of the truck was lettered. It said what? Benteen put his binoculars to his eyes:

TC LEISURELAND CONSTRUCTION
North Ambrose, Vermont

Terry was shouting something to the backhoe driver. Now Benteen brought up his walking stick and held it to his right shoulder, its length lying across his left arm. He put the end of the stick on Terry, right on his cowboy hat, and sighted down its length. Benteen felt like that fellow in the schoolbook warehouse all those years ago. Stop the process. Hit the brakes. Change the history. He felt like that fellow in Dallas, where Cordie's new girl's snake handling nemesis was this minute doing time.

Benteen said, *Bang.*

Only make-believe. Pretend. You can't stop it. There are no brakes. Benteen, sitting at the edge of his land and looking down his stick across to the loggers logging, the diggers digging, knew well he looked into the future. The future was that he might have been standing on 58th Street at the corner of Fifth Avenue with his back to Central Park. Before him the enormous city, foul, fuming, swarming, which covered the country in front of him, behind him, and on every side save only for the tiny green remnant of the park; all around it the buildings, the streets, the endless steel and stone, the pavement black, permanent, adamantine. And as for the park itself, that green instant, did anybody doubt that at last, when the city had need of it, it would be yielded up? The soft green remnant too would be engulfed.

Here they come. This is no drill, no drill, no drill.

"Fucking Rackstraw," said Hugh. "Fucking Dudley Do-right. He's waited all his life for this, you know? This is the high point, right here."

"What exactly was it that happened?" asked Mr. Townsend Higginbotham Guest.

"Terry got too fancy," said Hugh. "Well, we both did. We had the truck all fixed up. It looked like a load of logs. It *was* a load of logs. We built it up inside with, like, beams going across and short logs at the ends, and the shipment, you know, in the middle of it. We were ready to roll. Then Terry decided he'd rather not drive it down himself, and he got Kevin to do it, this kid who works for Terry's dad off and on. Course Kevin didn't know what was in the load, he just knew take it down to your place. He's only the driver."

"That was a good thought," said Mr. Guest.

"That was a bad thought," said Hugh. "Because Kevin's fucked up all the time. I mean, all the time. This guy is operating on about half a brain, the rest is smoke up there. He's out on 91 with the load, screaming along, swaying, rocking. Rackstraw makes him, gets after him, turns on his flashers, motions to Kevin to pull over.

"So fucking Kevin figures he'll run for it, right? In a log truck? *You'll never take me alive.* You know? By then he's so wasted he probably thought he was driving a spaceship. He cranks it up, *zoooom*. Rackstraw in hot pursuit."

"Good Lord," said Mr. Guest.

"They get to Brattleboro," Hugh said. "Kevin decides to get off 91. Mistake. He makes the ramp okay but then of course at, what is it, Route 9 there, you got a T. No way. He flips, loses the load, logs all over the place, the sidewalk, the street, people's yards. Logs everywhere. And guess what else?"

"Good Lord," said Mr. Guest.

"Rackstraw's right there. Comes up. Pulls Kevin out of the rig, roughs him up, too. Police brutality, no shit. Walks him over there, points to it, says, What's this? And Kevin— completely fucked up, now—Kevin looks at it and says, Wow, man, I don't know for sure but it looks to me like it might have been some kind of toy wagon. It belong to you?"

"Good Lord," said Mr. Guest. "Was anybody hurt?"

"No," said Hugh, "which is pretty much of a miracle. Kevin's got a court date next month. He's no problem about the shipment; he didn't know anything about it. His date's for driving under, driving to endanger, about fifty other things of that nature. Terry's dad's a little pissed, I guess, about the truck. Terry says he's going to have to kind of work on other things for the time being."

"What about the cart?" asked Mr. Guest.

"Totaled," said Hugh. "Rackstraw's got the pieces locked up out at the state police. It's evidence. He goes out there and jerks off onto it every couple of days. We'll never see it again."

"I trust not," said Mr. Guest.

"No problem," said Hugh. "Terry tells Rackstraw to talk to his lawyer, he don't know anything about anything. There's nothing there. But Terry's retired for now."

"Pity about the cart," said Mr. Guest.

"Fucking disaster," said Hugh.

"Mind your tongue, my boy," said Mr. Guest. "In any case, it could have been far worse. Be grateful. How do you feel?"

"Me?" said Hugh. "I feel great. Just great. That was a thousand bucks I didn't make."

"Well, well. On to other things. Feel ready for another adventure, do you?"

"Whoa," said Hugh. "That depends. No more big things. No more trucks."

"Absolutely not," said Mr. Guest. "Transport the weak link in the chain, clearly. I had in mind another, ah, project, though."

"At Garrett's?"

"Oh, yes," said Mr. Guest. "Where else? You've got a museum out there, my boy."

"What is it?"

"Nothing big," said Mr. Guest. "But a project that does present certain features of its own, certain problems of acquisition. It's an elegant business, really, done right."

"What?"

"Well," said Mr. Guest, "tell me: how are you about heights? You know: ladders, roofs, steeples, trees? Mind them, do you?"

Mr. Benteen had a small office in the barn for the farm paperwork, a snug, dusty room with a desk, a couple of files, a parlor stove, and two chairs for visitors. One of the chairs was halfway out the seat. The deputy sat on the other.

"All I'm asking you is what you really know about her," the deputy said.

"The same thing you know," Benteen said. "She's at Cordie's. She had some kind of trouble with some guy where she came from. She was trying to get away from him. She wound up at Cordie's. She works for Cordie at the inn. She had no part in taking that cart or the other stuff. You say you know who did. Go get them."

"I'm trying to conduct an investigation, here," the deputy said. "I'd think you'd cooperate. You're the one getting ripped off. Have you ever had her out here?"

"Why?" Benteen said. "What the hell business is that of yours?"

"Well, more than you think, maybe," the deputy said. "You think we don't know the way you carried on out here, still carry on? The girls? I hope they're all over eighteen."

"You're a fool," said Benteen.

"Look," the deputy said. "This ain't why I'm here, all right? Those girls, women, what they do out here is their business. They don't know any better, I can't help them. I'm conducting a routine police investigation, for theft. Now. This girl of Cordie's. Has she been here?"

"No."

"Then there's no way you know she could know about the cart in the shed down at the other place?"

"No."

"Well, okay, then," said the deputy.

"I thought you had a line on Terry and some other fellow. Some big thief."

"The investigation is ongoing," the deputy said. "I don't want to comment at this time."

"You sound like a god damned lawyer, you know that?" Benteen said.

"Look," the deputy said. "Let's be realistic. She's new in town. Nobody really knows her or anything about her except that she's mixed up with bad people out of state. What I mean, she's a stranger. Now, somebody took your cart. Whoever it was was at least two people, at least one of them knew your place. So we check her out. Is she a suspect? Not yet. Are we interested in her? You bet we are."

"Get out of here," said Benteen. "Go talk to Cordie, you want to know about her girl."

"She isn't real cooperative," the deputy said.

"I'll bet she isn't," Benteen said. "I'll bet she liked to thrown you right out of there. Hah. I'll just bet she ain't cooperative."

"She acts like she's got to protect those girls she takes in," the deputy said. "Most of them aren't worth protecting. They're no damned good, a lot of them. They were, they wouldn't be in trouble. It's like I said a minute ago. They asked for trouble, most of them. They got it. If they were any good they wouldn't be at her place at all."

"Like this particular one, you think," Benteen said.

"I told you," the deputy said. "I'm trying to conduct an investigation. I'm investigating a robbery. Your robbery. That's my job."

"Go do your job someplace else," Benteen said. "Go on."

The Vermont moose, then, a creature of myth, of legend, a marvel that nevertheless plainly exists and is to be seen going about in the world, and yet is no less a marvel for its reality: as though you could meet a dinosaur on a village street or hit one with your car. A creature, what's more, utterly impossible in the Vermont whose image is fixed in the idealizing minds, forever opposed, of Mr. Benteen and the younger Condosta—a venue, in the one case, amounting to a kind of post-agricultural deer park, in the other to a suburb of noplace. Unthinkable, the moose, in either of the settings whose way is being prepared, yet it is with us now: a creature not of open, productive land, and not of the subdivision, but of the wilderness—no, stranger than that, a traveler from another epoch entirely, a Pleistocene survivor, less a modern animal than one of the hairy beasts of the Ice Age: the mastodon, the saber-toothed cat, the great Irish elk. This former farm district, not yet fully declined to whatever its lesser condition is to be, has been visited by a last magnificent anachronism.

The damndest most peculiar looking thing, too: a flat-horn deer, huge, in appearance a cross between a Clydesdale and a camel. Lacking the clownish humanity of the bear, the motion of the deer, or the keenness of the predators, it has instead repose, a vast, peaceable indifference. The moose in Vermont passes across your vision placidly, in no hurry, like a sailing ship, like a cloud shadow.

Still following its four or five deer, it crossed the path no more than thirty feet in front of Benteen. The deer bounded ahead into the woods, but the moose stopped in the path. It regarded him. Benteen waited. It was black, the size of a small garage. It must be the same one Marvin saw, there can't be more than one.

Marvin would be after it, too. He'd be asking for the African rifle, the shoulder-buster. Benteen's father, old Guy, had been a hunter of big game, in fact in his time a kind of tinhorn Teddy Roosevelt. He'd shot a moose in Canada whose head to this day hung in the barroom of the Benedict House, watching over the drunks, reformed and otherwise. Old Guy's African rifle, a .505 Gibbs, an elephant gun, stood in its cabinet at the house. The rifle was a custom job, bought by the old man in London as though it had been a suit of clothes, fitted to him like a suit of clothes, too. He'd been on his way out to Kenya. Sometime before the war: 1935? 1936? What a picture: the old fraud out there on those dusty plains amongst the unending movement of the game, the gazelles, the wildebeests, the buffalo, the lions, living it up in his safari outfit, in the care of some sunburned mountebank of an Englishman, scapegrace second son of minor barony in subalcoholic exile beneath Kilimanjaro: twenty-five black fellows, a Land Rover, a tent the size of a small barn, and two hundred cases of gin—the whole show hired out of Nairobi for, what, fifty bucks a day?

The moose went on into the woods. For all its size, the second it left the path it vanished. There was no noise of its progress through the woods, no footfalls, no cracking of the brush. Remarkable how such a big thing can move so silently.

In 1925 old Guy had traveled to British Columbia to kill the barroom moose. What would he think today of shooting one out of his own backyard?

Well, after that her or Tommy would bring him his coffee and brandy and by that time the dining room would be mostly empty. She'd be getting it set for next day. I'd help her. Garrett sat there with his coffee and brandy.

Have one with me, he said.

No, thank you very much, I said.

What about you, Tex? he said.

Not her, either, I said. She's on duty. All I need is for some guest to smell drink on the girls.

If you want to buy me a drink, she said to Garrett, you're going to have to take me someplace nice.

What does that mean? I said.

I don't know, Garrett said. You might move too quick for me. It's a known fact you're a thief.

They had been going back and forth that way. Garrett had started out talking about Buddy Rackstraw, the sheriff's deputy. He'd been to see Garrett. He was investigating the antiques gone missing from Garrett's.

I had to laugh.

Buddy Rackstraw, I said, couldn't investigate a road-killed cat.

Cordie don't have no opinion at all of Deputy Rackstraw, Garrett told the girl.

Neither do I, she said. He brought me here when I first came.

He's after you, Garrett said. He thinks you're the one swiped granny's old pony cart. Was that you?

It sure was, she said.

Deputy's right, then, Garrett said. Where did you put it?

I hid it in my underwear, she said.

God's sake, I said. Be careful. That kind of talk, you'll get the old boy all revved up. I don't know if his heart will stand it.

Nothing wrong with my heart, Garrett said.

I thought that was Terry, I said. I thought it was on one of their trucks. Buddy doesn't really think she's in on that. Does he?

Says he does, Garrett said. He's checking you out because you're a stranger. You might be part of some big antique-stealing ring, he says.

If I was, would I be working here? she asked.

Wait a minute, I said. What's the matter with working here?

Well, Garrett said. You'd be under cover.

Under whose covers? she said. Under your covers?

You see what I mean? Garrett said. I'm afraid she'd move too fast for me.

Ummm, I said.

I wish I still had that cart, though, Garrett was saying. It was a pretty thing, too. Not much bigger than an armchair, made of basketwork, all shiny. Made in France. My mother rode around in it when she was just a little girl, it was made to be pulled by a pony or even a big dog. I got an old picture of her in it, sitting there. They had a pony to it and she's all dressed up in some kind of fancy outfit to look like an Italian boatman. A gondolier, I swear to God. Who'd steal such a thing?

Anybody who thought he knew where he could sell it, it looks like, I said.

A pony? she said. There was a pony to pull it?

That's right, Garrett said. A little thing like a Shetland pony. I wish I still had that cart. I do. I'd get it out, take you for a ride.

You would? she said. Where to?

Just around, Garrett said. Here and there.

Would I have to dress up like a gondolier? she said.

You could dress any way you wanted, Garrett said.

You got a pony to pull us? she asked him.

I'll get one, Garrett said.

No, she said. No ponies.

Hugh loaded the dump truck in the woodyard at Benteens'. It took him the whole day, since as it happened he was by himself. Marvin was mowing again. Fourth of July: they were starting the second cutting. He might just as well have held off a day and helped Hugh with Vergil's wood, but Benteen said no. Benteen wanted Hugh to have to load the wood alone, every stick. He'd intended it that way all along. He knew it, and Hugh knew it. Hugh didn't mind. As long as he was sticking it to Benteen, he didn't mind. It was as though Hugh were fucking Benteen's wife: because of that, he could put up with a good deal from Benteen. Besides, it wasn't going to last much longer, was it? He'd be gone.

A mountain of firewood, his to move all by himself, like a kid in a fairy tale. He tossed the heavy chunks up in an arc that brought them down into the dump truck's bed with a bang. Hugh made a game of it at first: he was a cannon, a mortar, each chunk a shell in its high, steep path, higher, steeper than was necessary. *Whump. Bang.* He made a game of the job, but it was no game. After an hour Hugh quit and climbed up the side of the dump bed to see how fast it was filling up. The bed looked like a dry swimming pool with seven dead fish at the bottom. He was into a long day here.

He finished about six. Wood was visible above the sides of the dump bed. Benteen had said to take the load out to Vergil's the next day, so Hugh would have daylight for stacking it. Hugh had other plans. He climbed up into the cab and started up.

Pulling the truck into Vergil's lane, he immediately hung the high dump box up on a branch of one of the trees that crowded so close to the lane. Hugh didn't care: if Benteen wanted him to drive that thing in there and hadn't gotten around to clearing the way, that was his problem. Hugh punched it and was glad to hear the branch give way with a loud ripping and then a bad crack like a rifle shot. So much for that tree. He made it to Vergil's dooryard without doing any more damage.

In the yard Hugh got it turned around and backed up to Vergil's shed, which adjoined the house, right in front. He stopped then and got down to take out the pins from the rear gate so the load would dump when he raised the box.

Althea came out of the house, running.

"Can you come in?" she said to Hugh. "I know you don't want to. Can you come? Can you come in now? We got trouble here. I need you."

"What?" Hugh said.

"He's down," Althea said. "He can't get up. I can't get him up. Come in here now."

She turned and started back to the house. Hugh followed her. Vergil had died, he thought. Vergil was dead in there, and in a second he'd be with him, he'd be looking at him. Hugh looked back to the lane, the yard, the truck, but Althea was at the door.

"In here," she said.

In a corner of the kitchen, on the floor, Vergil lay curled up with his knees under his chin. He wasn't dead, but he wasn't moving. When Althea and Hugh came near him he turned his head to look at them. He nodded to them.

"I was out back," Althea said. "Came in and found him. Must be he tried to get out of his chair, didn't make it. He's okay. Thing is, curled up the way he is, I can't get him straightened out so as to get him up."

"What's wrong with him?" Hugh asked.

"He kind of seizes up, like," Althea said.

"What do you want to do?" Hugh said.

"Well," said Althea, "you get his legs. We'll just see if we can't pull him straight, get him up. Come on, old man. You're all right."

So Hugh knelt at Vergil's feet, took hold of his ankles. Vergil's skin was white as milk there, and the big leg bones that Hugh had to grip were sharp and hard. Althea took Vergil under the arms, and together they tried to turn him on his back and make him lie extended.

"He don't want to come," said Althea.

Vergil didn't resist, but he didn't relax. He watched Hugh at his feet calmly, as though Hugh were a shoe clerk fitting him with a new pair of boots. Vergil showed no pain, but he wouldn't or couldn't straighten his legs. Hugh pulled a little harder. Vergil didn't give.

"Hold it," said Althea. She let go of Vergil's arms. "This ain't the way. What are you doing here, old boy?"

"He's all wet," Hugh said. Vergil was wearing a suit of long underwear under a bathrobe. Hugh could see where he'd wet himself around the middle.

"Is that it?" said Althea. "Is that it? Yes, it is. He must have been going for his piss bottle. Why didn't you knock for me? I'd have fixed you up. That's right: I was out back. Poor old boy."

"Why won't he let go?" Hugh said.

"He don't want you to see," said Althea. "How'd you feel, grown man, pissed yourself? Look, old boy, we got to get you fixed up here. Don't worry about this. We don't mind."

Oh, is that right?

She took Vergil under his arms again, and again Hugh tried to draw his ankles out, but still Vergil held onto his curl.

"Fuck this," Hugh said. "Where do you want him?"

"Bedroom, I guess," said Althea.

Hugh put down Vergil's ankles and got up on one knee beside him. He took Vergil under the knees and shoulders and stood easily, lifting Vergil lightly in his arms.

"Well, look at you," said Althea.

"Where is it?" Hugh asked. Althea pointed to a door at the end of the kitchen. She started for it. Hugh followed, carrying Vergil in front of him, at his chest, like a young bride. He could feel the wet of Vergil's soaking robe and now he could smell the piss.

Althea waited at the bedroom door.

"You got him okay?" she asked.

"He don't weigh nothing," Hugh said.

He laid Vergil on his narrow bed. Vergil then stretched out a little and rolled onto his back. He tried to gather his robe at the front.

"That's better," said Althea.

Hugh stood beside the bed. He wondered if there was someplace he could wash Vergil's piss off him. There wasn't, unless he stayed here. It was more important to get out. Althea was taking Vergil's robe off him. Vergil was letting her. In a minute he'd be lying there naked.

"Well, I guess that's it," said Hugh.

"Long as you're here," said Althea from Vergil's bedside, "think you could give me a hand with his underwear?"

* * *

Hugh fired out of Vergil's front door as though he'd been shot from the house. In the yard he took a deep breath of the clean air. He ran to the truck, started up, and got it into gear. He jerked out of the yard and into the lane. In the lane Hugh saw ahead of him, hanging by a livid white splinter over the roadway, the torn branch he'd broken on the way in. He stopped. He'd never dumped the wood.

Motherfucker, Hugh said. Oh, motherfuckermother.

Violently he reversed it all the way back up the lane and into the yard. He put the box up to the shed, jumped down, shot the pins behind, jumped back up into the seat, and threw the dump lever. The wood poured down out of the box with a roar. Hugh let the box down. He didn't get out to clear the box of the last chunks. He didn't get out to pin the rear gate. He put the truck in gear and rolled out of there as fast as he could, the heavy gate of the truck flapping and banging on the bumps.

Back at the house Althea came out to the yard as Hugh drove into the lane. He didn't see her. Althea waved after him.

"Thanks," she called. "Thanks a lot. I'll tell him you did good."

Who reads all these books? she asked. You read all these? she asked Garrett.

It must have been twenty years since I was in that room, what Garrett's father called the book room—off the kitchen there at Benteens'. Well, I hadn't been inside the house at all in that time. When I'd be the one to drive Garrett home, I'd drop him at the side and go on. But this night he asked us both to come in and we went. We went ahead. Hugh was off somewhere, I don't know, he wasn't driving, so I said I'd drop Garrett. We'd got done in the dining room, I'd locked the bar down about nine and come for him there at his table to drive him home. Her I'd planned to have wait and I'd pick her up on my way back from dropping Garrett.

Ask her to ride along, he said.

No need, I said. I'll get her on my way back.

Ask her, he said.

So the three of us went out to Benteens' and when we pulled in there he said Come in for a bit and I hadn't been in the house in maybe not twenty years but certainly fifteen. Course it was dark, but Garrett went first and put on the outside light and we went in through the kitchen with that wide old fireplace and the big blue stove and Garrett turned the light on and kind of stood and let us go in and I went across the kitchen and looked into the book room. She came up beside me and Garrett came and reached around the doorway and turned on the light in there. He hadn't fixed it up, changed it at all: there were bookcases right from the floor up to the ceiling all around. There must have been several hundred books.

You read all these? she asked.

Not me, Garrett said. Cordie's dad's the only one who ever read them all.

I don't mind saying I was keen on seeing inside that house. When I was a girl it was the biggest house I'd ever been in, though it wasn't all that big. The kitchen was big, but the book room wasn't all that big and the little bedroom beside it wasn't much more than a bed and a chest of drawers and room to stand up. No chair, no table. Garrett had himself moved in there. It looked as though he lived pretty much in the kitchen and the book room and bedroom. The other rooms off the kitchen, the front rooms, were closed up, and you couldn't tell about the upstairs. He was all by himself in the house, of course, he didn't need anywhere near the room. Still, I didn't like to think of him letting the place go down, though what we saw looked kept up enough. Garrett's neat. Give him that. Orderly.

I ought to sell them, he said. He and her were still in the book room. I was kind of looking around the rest of the first floor. Except for the shut-up rooms, nothing was changed.

I ought to sell them off, Garrett said. The mice are eating them all up.

You sell those books, you'll answer to me, I called out to them.

Oh, is that right? Garrett said.

Believe it, I said. We were going back and forth that way.

I think I will sell them, Garrett said. You set such store by them, maybe I'll sell them to you.

You won't sell them to nobody, I said.

I think I will sell them to you, at that, Garrett said. That boy of yours can have them. Wonder Boy. He's a studying kid.

At that the girl laughed.

He's not a studying kid? Garrett asked her.

Oh, he's studying something, she said.

What's he studying? Garrett said.

Not books, she said.

What, then? Garrett said. But she'd left the book room and looked into his little bedroom. Who are these? she asked. She meant the old photographs Garrett had on his chest of drawers in there. She went right to them, picked one up, and held it. She showed it to me. Who are they?

Where did this come from? I asked Garrett. I'd never seen it before.

I've had it, he said.

That's his father, him, and my father, I told her.

There they were, the two boys and the old man. They were standing in front of an open barn door, the same barn right outside here, the photo dark in the barn but bright outside, too bright—it wasn't much of a picture, just a snapshot. The sun was in their eyes, they were grinning into the sun, the boys both taller than Garrett's father, both blond from the summer sun. Lined up: Garrett, the old man, Daddy. Who took that picture? Who would have been around that day?

That's you? the girl said. She put her finger on the picture.

Garrett looked at it. That's me take away about fifty years, he said.

Fifty? she said.

Don't tell him how young he looks, I said. We got to go.

But she had hold of another picture, the one of the girl in the pony cart, Garrett's mother it was, kind of an old brown picture of this little girl sitting up there in the cart—just two wheels, not much more than a sulky.

That's the cart that got stolen, she said.

That's it, Garrett said. That's Mamma and that's the cart.

There's that little pony, I said.

There he is, Garrett said. She didn't say anything.

Don't you like ponies? Garrett asked her.

Sure, she said. Sure, I like them.

Think of that little girl in the picture from years ago. How many? Pretty near a hundred, it must be. Her all dressed up in a kind of pinafore and a flat straw hat with a ribbon to it, looking solemn like they always do in pictures from back then. They never smile.

Later in the car she said, You're kind of quiet. You okay?

The fact is, so was she. So was she quiet.

Yes, I said, I'm quiet. Enjoy it while you can.

You sure? she said.

I'm sure.

But that other picture, of the three of them, the two boys and that strange old man, Daddy and Garrett and him, that old-time thing, when it sneaks up on you like that, when it surprises you, is mostly sad, isn't it? Why? Nothing that terrible happened. It's just that when you don't think about it and then you do, it's all so long ago.

If you drive into Ambrose, Vermont, from the east you will come over Diamond Mountain and then drop down into the little valley of the Dead River. About at the height of the mountain the road bends south, and from a wide place up there where the snowplows turn around you can see for an instant all the way down the valley almost to the village, a matter of, say, five miles.

Make the drive early on a fair summer morning, and you will certainly see, from the overlook up on the mountain, the sunlight flashing off a bright object far ahead down the valley. It might be the windows of a house catching the light, except that the reflection seems to come from a wooded belt to the west of the village and so, you understand, must be produced by an object set at least as high as the treetops. You go on around the bend and in a second you have lost it, but what you saw flashing in the sun was the great weather vane that surmounts the barn cupola at Mr. Benteen's place: a golden ram.

Seventy feet in the air, above all but the oldest trees, up there almost with the top of the village steeple, the ram surveyed the country, creaking on its iron pivot. It was five feet long, made of tin, painted gold. The figure of the ram was elongated, clumsy, indeed absurd. It didn't look like a sheep; it looked most like an enormous dachshund. It was mounted on an arrow to indicate the wind direction. The arrow bore the embossed date 1844, quite invisible from the ground. The weather vane was an artifact of the period when that whole country had gone in for sheep raising. It was far older than the barn. It had originally stood atop a smaller barn that had burned around 1890. Benteens then built the present barn, a majestic structure, a cathedral of a barn, and set the antique ram on its lofty perch. About every five years a steeplejack came over from New Hampshire to paint the steeple of the church in North Ambrose. When he was done, he'd go on to Benteens' and give the ram a coat of gilt.

The golden ram caught the morning sun only around midsummer. Other times of the year the angle of light was wrong, apparently. In June, however, July, it made a landmark for those arriving in the town from the east and was seen with some affection by anyone who knew the meaning of the bright light down the valley, a group that included Mr. Townsend Higginbotham Guest, the private dealer.

Mr. Guest had spent twenty good years patiently driving the roads into the hills with the rising sun at his back, looking for exactly such flashing beams. To him they meant one thing. Mr. Guest had a customer outside Atlanta who specialized in weather vanes that represented animals, and he knew an incurious collector in Palm Springs who would take any weather vane Mr. Guest sent him as long as Mr. Guest, whose probity was absolute, attested it came from somewhere in the state of Vermont.

Mr. Guest took particular care over weather vanes. He had an approach to them that was quite his own. When he happened on one he hadn't seen before, for example Benteens' golden ram, he would locate it and then examine it using a telescope he kept for that purpose. If the ram looked promising, if it was old, if it had an unusual form, he would photograph it with a long lens. Mr. Guest would then return to Boston, where he would have a ram about the size he judged Benteens' to be cut out of aluminum sheet stock by a metal fabricator in Mattapan and gilded by an automobile body shop in Cambridge. The cost to Mr. Guest might be $100.

When the work was done he'd go back into the country with his new ram and wait until the middle of a favorable night, when he'd climb up the barn, take the old ram, put the new one in its place, and leave. He knew the odds were greatly against anyone's ever realizing the original ram was gone. Side by side with the genuine ram, his cheap forgery wouldn't pass for a minute, but up on top of the barn, seventy feet in the air, one was as good as the other. The perfect theft is the undetected theft. Weather vanes, handled properly, were a safe thing, the equivalent in Mr. Guest's line, perhaps, of telephone stock.

Mr. Guest's weather vanes were to be seen all up and down the state from Massachusetts clear to the Canadian border. There was a splendid Guest catamount atop a grange hall in Arlington, a curiously wrought Guest dragon on a barn outside St. Johnsbury. There had even been a Guest scholar, in gown and mortarboard, on the belfry of one of the academic buildings at Middlebury College. That one was gone, however. Boisterous students had recently contrived to steal it, never guessing it had been stolen long before their time.

Now past middle age, Mr. Guest faced two difficulties: so long had he been at the weather vane trade in Vermont, and to such good purpose, that he began to fear going after his own works; and he was certainly too old for scaling barns, towers, steeples. The first difficulty Mr. Guest met confidently, with a memory made strong in early life through a sound Latin education. The second had led him in recent years to recruit. Fortunately Mr. Guest had always had a way with the young. Well, some of them.

"God damn it," Benteen said. "You dumped it. You dumped it and left. You expect her to handle all that? I told you to stack it. That was the job. You didn't do the job. She can't hump a cord of wood by herself. Look at her. Open up your eyes and look at her. She needs help. They need help out there, do you understand that? Do you understand anything?"

"Wait a minute," said Hugh.

"I won't wait a minute," Benteen said. "What's the matter with you? I gave you a job to do. Can't you hear?"

"He was like passed out when I got there," said Hugh. "He was passed out on the floor. She couldn't move him. I moved him. We got him around. I forgot about the wood. I thought he'd died."

"He was what?"

"Passed out. Not passed out. I don't know: he was curled up on the floor. She couldn't move him. She asked me to get him into the other room."

"What was the matter with him?"

"I don't know. How are you supposed to know? He's three-quarters dead as it is. He'd pissed himself, all over. All over the floor. He was a fucking mess. She asked me to get him to his bed."

"And you did it?"

"I did."

"How?"

"I picked him up and carried him."

"You did? You carried him?"

"Sure. He don't weigh nothing. He's like a bunch of sticks in there."

"Then what?"

"Then we got him out of his clothes and she started to get him cleaned up. I left. I forgot about the wood."

"Is he all right?"

"He was when I left. I guess. As much as he ever is. Look, I forgot about the wood. Then I remembered, I went back. It was nearly dark so I dumped it. What did you want me to do, drive it back here and take it out there all over again? I'll go back sometime and get it in the shed for her."

"Tomorrow," Benteen said. "Not sometime. Tomorrow. You don't leave it for her to do."

"I said I would," said Hugh.

"You leave it, she'll do it herself," Benteen said.

"I thought you said she couldn't."

"She can't," said Benteen. "Don't you understand anything? What's the matter with you?"

"I'll do it," said Hugh.

"You're god damned right you will," Benteen said. "You'll get yourself back out there tomorrow and stack every stick in the shed for her. You won't quit 'til it's all in."

"I said I would," said Hugh. "I said I would and I will."

"Do you understand me now?" Benteen asked him.

"Yes, I understand you."

"You do?" said Benteen. "You do? Because you didn't before. You had, you wouldn't just drive in there and dump it and drive off like some kind of god damned mailman. You were there to help. I pay you to help. The last weeks you haven't been here. You've been on the moon."

"You don't like the way I do my work," said Hugh. "You can fire me."

"Fire you?"

"That's right. Go ahead. Fire me."

"No," said Benteen.

"Go ahead," Hugh said.

"No," said Benteen. "You do the work I give you to do and do it the way I tell you to do it. That's all. You don't have to like it, you just have to do it."

It might have been a week after the time out at Garrett's, I left the inn to go home for supper and when I got into my car there was Garrett sitting in the passenger's seat. I got right in beside him before I saw him there.

You liked to scared me half to death, I said. What do you think you're doing?

Waiting for you, he said. Go ahead, drive.

You want to go home? I said. It's not even five.

No, he said. Drive around.

So I started the car and we drove through the village and out along the river. Anyplace, the way he said.

Your girl, Garrett said.

And I thought, Oh, boy.

She's moving out to my place, he said. She'll be coming with me.

Is that right? I said.

I need her, Garrett said. I need a driver.

Hugh's your driver, I said.

He's on the moon, Garrett said. He's never around. You can't find him, he's not doing his work, he's off dreaming. Something's going on with him. He's on the moon half the time. Let Marv have him. I need another one. Driver. Anyway, I'm sick of talking to myself out there. I'm all by myself out there. You don't know.

Don't I? I thought. But I shut up. I said, By yourself? What do you mean? There's Marv. There's Hugh. LeRoy. The others. God's sake, you've practically got an army with you out there.

You know what I mean, he said.

Well, I said, I don't know what you want from me. She's a grownup. She can do what she wants.

You're looking out for her, Garrett said.

I am not, I said. Have you asked her?

No, Garrett said.

You planning on asking her? I said. Or are you just going to come in and, like, sweep her away?

Look, Garrett said. I'm trying to do the right thing here.

I had to laugh.

What about her boyfriend? I said. What are you going to do about him?

Nothing, Garrett said. He'll never come up here.

I hope not, I said.

Never, Garrett said.

I don't know what Hugh's going to do, I said. If she moves out there. They're, uh . . .

It don't matter, Garrett said. I need her. If I ask her, she'll come. You know she will.

Yes, I said. I expect she will.

It's no game, Garrett said then. It's no game over there. It's no drill.

What? I said. I didn't know what he was talking about.

Nothing, Garrett said. I don't know. The last couple of weeks. I don't know. Getting older.

Not getting any smarter, though, I said. I can see that.

No, well, it don't pay to get too smart, Garrett said. Come to that, you're smart enough for the both of us. What

I ought to do, what I ought to do is leave her alone and get you out there with me. How would that be?

Hah, I said.

Mr. Benteen let his right hand down to rest on the dog's head. Idly he scratched its ears, its shoulders.

"Deputy thinks she's in it," he said. "He thinks she and Terry got the cart. He says there's some kind of ring that they're part of."

Marvin didn't say anything. He and Benteen sat in the yard behind the house where Marvin lived, a cottage, really, half a mile past the big house, Benteens'. They sat on wooden chairs, the dog on the grass between them.

"You think he's right?" Benteen asked.

"You were missing stuff before she came," said Marvin.

"Nothing that big," said Benteen. "Deputy thinks Terry had to had help on that."

"Don't make it her," said Marvin.

"You think there's a ring, the way he says?" Benteen asked.

"I don't know why not," Marvin said. "There's everything else."

Marvin made the chairs they sat on. They were Adirondack chairs, made of simple pine boards assembled to give you a fair amount of lean-back when you sat, maybe too much lean-back. Marvin had a table saw set up in his kitchen. He made the chairs there in his spare time. Marvin's Adirondack chairs were all over his house and yard, fifteen or twenty of them. They weren't very comfortable, but then you didn't have to sit on them.

"She's running away from some madman," Benteen said. "He's in jail in Texas. He'll be after her. He's supposed to be a piece of work. She's afraid he'll show up here. You know about that?"

"I heard."

"What do you think?"

"Well," said Marvin, "he ain't yet."

"Cordie says Wonder Boy's got her," said Benteen.

They didn't look at each other as they spoke, and they weren't in any hurry. They might have been watching a game or other event unfold before them, they might have been gazing out over tennis courts, over the empty ocean. They sat side by side on the hard chairs in back of Marvin's. Before them was twenty feet of grass, then Marvin's little vegetable garden, then Marvin's pear trees, then the woods.

"You think he is?" Benteen asked.

"Somebody's got somebody," said Marvin. "He acts like he's short of sleep, too. Stumbling around."

"I had her up to the house the other night," Benteen said.

"Uh-huh," Marvin said.

"The thing is, she's a kid," Benteen said.

"Some want kids," Marvin said. "Most do."

"Not me," said Benteen.

Marvin's dog had been lying on the grass between them, under Benteen's hand. Now it raised its head, pointed its ears. It looked intently down the yard toward the garden. The dog sighed. Some animal must be moving back there, a rabbit, a chuck.

"That big guy was up there again this morning," Marvin said. "I saw him. Same place. Same deer with him. I thought I might take a walk up there one day."

"I was thinking of talking to her," Benteen said.

"I thought I might take that old .505 rifle," Marvin said.

"Shaky," Benteen said. "The last couple of weeks. It's no game, you know. It's no drill."

"I thought I might take it up there tomorrow," Marvin said. "Tomorrow, the next day."

Benteen nodded.

"Pretty shaky," he said. "Haven't been sleeping good."

"You want to take it slow," Marvin said.

"You seen that new job of Condostas'?" Benteen asked him.

"No," Marvin said.

"You ought to see it," Benteen said. "There's a house. He's putting a god damned house in there. We'll go over there. You ought to see it."

"All right," said Marvin.

Marvin looked down at the dog. Its head was up. It was sniffing the air.

"You want me to talk to her?" Marvin said.

"No," said Benteen. "I will."

The dog's nose sought in the air. It pulsed in the air like a little heart.

"Must be there's something out there," Marvin said.

"You aren't thinking about going out there, are you?"

"I might be. I haven't been invited."

"What if you were? Would you go?"

"Yes."

"Why?"

"Why not? Why shouldn't I?"

"Why should you? What do you get? You think he likes you? He won't even know you're there, except maybe while he's fucking you. Probably not even then."

"Not like you."

"No: not like me. Nothing like me."

"Forget it. Just forget it."

"Hey, your life, okay? I don't get it, that's all. Is it because he's rich? Because he's rich and everybody treats him like he's important?"

"I said forget it."

"Listen, Garrett doesn't care about you. He don't need a girlfriend, he needs a keeper. You're so curious about Garrett? Okay, I'll tell you: Garrett's a rich guy who doesn't have any idea what's going on. The world's full of them. Garrett's ours. That's all. You think he's going to, what, marry you and leave you all his money when he dies?"

"No."

"Then why? Hulon? You think you're safer from him out at Garrett's?"

"Maybe."

"You think Garrett could take on Hulon?"

"There's others out there with him. You, Marvin, others."

"Not me. Not for long."

"No?"

"I know what it is. What it is is you're going there to whore for that crazy old guy just because you think he's your best shot. You think you're moving up. That's what it is."

"So what is that to you? What are you that's any different?"

"Your friend. I'm your friend."

"Come on. You're no different from what you say he is. All you want to do is fuck."

"Sure, I do. So what? So do you. Don't you? Can't I fuck you and be your friend?"

"I don't know."

"Okay. Listen. You're afraid of Hulon. Or maybe you aren't. Maybe you just want to make a move. Okay. Here's what I'll do. I've got something coming in, the next couple of weeks. Upwards of a thousand dollars, closer to two. I got a car. We'll go. We'll go someplace else, get set up."

"What are you talking about, something coming in?"

"Look, I'll tell you what it is: I can't do it here any more. I mean, it's fine, but I can't do it. Marv? He's a fine guy. I've known him all my life. If I have to listen to him one more day? Garrett? If I have to pitch his hay and dig his holes one more day? Vergil? If I have to go out and watch Vergil whipping his hound one more day? If I have to sit down at the table here and eat with my mom one more day? I can't do it. I'll bust. I'll die. That money comes in and I'm gone. What I'm saying to you is: come too."

"Where do you get money like that?"

"Things. Things I've got working. I'll tell you all about it another time. Point is, I'm going. Come with me."

"That's nice."

"Course it is. I'm a nice guy."

"That's nice, but I don't think so."

"Why not?"

"I like it here."

Well, he asked her right out, Garrett did: Have you ever been married? You want to marry me?

Sat at his table with his brandy and watched her and me work, talking back and forth, and came right to it like that: You want to marry me?

She didn't miss a step, I'll give her that. What are you calling marriage? she asked him. What do you mean by marriage?

It started out they were talking about driving and Garrett's fancy new car. He'd been looking for a new driver, he said. Hugh wasn't driving him any more.

Why not? she asked him. What's the matter?

He don't tend to business, Garrett said.

He doesn't? she said. Not to your business, maybe.

To yours? Garrett said.

My business is right here, she said. I just help out around here.

You're wasted, Garrett said.

What do you mean, wasted? I said.

She's wasted, Garrett said. You know how to drive?

I drove myself up here to you all, didn't I? she said.

That's right, Garrett said. What did you drive?

Eighty-one Olds, she said. Belongs to Hulon's mom. Needs some work, now, a lot of work. Expensive work.

Don't bother, Garrett said. Get rid of it. You ever driven a real car?

Oh, I said, like yours, I guess.

That's right, Garrett said. Mercedes-Benz, a good big one. Get yourself a German car, every time. The Germans, when they're making cars, pretend they're still making tanks, bombers, battleships, so every car comes off the line with something extra. They build the hell out of them. Best car in the world. Drives like you're driving along in your own living room. You'll see.

I will? she said. I don't know if I will or not. I'm a plain old girl from Fort Worth, you know? I'm not used to fancy things.

You'll take right to them, Garrett said. People do. You'd be surprised.

We were putting out clean tablecloths for the next day. She'd throw out a tablecloth, flap it out, then let it settle down onto the table. She's looking at what she's doing. He's looking at her.

Besides, she said, what if I ran that fancy car too hard? I might break it down. I might burn out a bearing, or something.

Yes, I said to Garrett. You got to think about that, don't you? She might run it too hot.

You can't run that car too hard, Garrett said. I told you, they build them too strong over there.

Still, I said, you got to worry about that, an expensive car and all.

You girls let me worry about the car, Garrett said. The car's mine. You're just the driver.

I don't know, she said. I haven't said I would.

Say it, Garrett said.

I'll think about it, she said.

You do that, Garrett said. You ever been married?

No.

You want to marry me?

Oh, boy, I thought. And she didn't miss a beat. She flapped out another tablecloth and said something like, What do you mean by marriage? And Garrett told her.

Marriage? What does anybody mean? You're a stranger here. Law's after you. Snake-handler's after you. You're stuck working this crummy job. (Hah.) You need protection. You need a place to go. I got a place. I need a driver. You be my driver. I'll give you a place to go. Fair exchange. What else is marriage?

What do you mean, crummy job? I said.

What do you mean, driver? she said.

Driver, Garrett said. You drive me where I want to go.

Where's that? she asked him.

Where ain't your concern, Garrett said.

Yeah, well, I'll think it over, she said.

You do that, Garrett said. You think it right through. Think it through good. Think it through quick.

That was how he put it to her that night. Not real eloquent. Not a lot of flowers and violins for Garrett. He pretty much came straight out with it. He said he would and he did. She'll think it over, but Garrett had told me, If I ask her, she'll come, and I expect he's right. She'll figure, Why not? She don't know, though she'll find out. Altogether, it ain't much of a match, but then it don't have to last any longer than anybody wants it to, does it? So I'm willing to look on the bright side and not look too hard. It's a marriage, kind of, and Daddy said, whenever there was a wedding, he said, Let me not to the marriage of true impediments admit minds.

The deputy was talking as though he'd about had enough.

"Look," he said. "I'm asking for your cooperation. You understand: I don't have to do that. I'm conducting an investigation, here. I can enter your place to do that."

"The hell you can," Benteen said. "Not without a court order, you can't. This ain't Russia. Not yet."

"All I'm going to do is sit and wait for him. You won't even know I'm here. I want to be here when he comes."

"What happened to the girl?" Benteen said. "You were after the girl."

"She's clear," said the deputy. "We're talking about Wonder Boy. Nobody else."

"You're crazy," Benteen said. "Kid's a jerk but he's not a thief."

"Look," said the deputy. "We had a break. New information. From down country. I can't tell you much about it but we know a lot more about your case than we did even last week. We know he's the one at this end. Him and Terry but mostly him."

"You don't know anything of the kind," said Benteen. "What new information? You've got a doper kid says maybe he was around with Terry. You've got that he's got a smart mouth. You've got that you don't like him. What else have you got? What new information?"

"I told you," said the deputy. "I can't get into that with you at this time. But somebody is working this from in here. Anybody can see that. Anybody but you. Your own guy has been robbing you. How do you feel about that? What does that mean to you? Don't you want to do something about that?"

"Somebody has been robbing me," said Benteen.

"What do you mean?" the deputy asked him. "Who?"

"Somebody," said Benteen. "Somebody has been robbing me. But not him, and not here."

"I don't know what you're talking about," the deputy said.

"I know you don't," Benteen said. "You don't know what I'm talking about. You don't know a god damned thing except that you don't like that kid. That's all you know. Leave him alone. Christ, you're supposed to be an officer of the law. What happened to being innocent until they prove you guilty?"

"Yeah," said the deputy. "Yeah, well, that's for in court, you know? I'm a cop. Far as I'm concerned, you're guilty whether they prove it or not."

"Keep off my place," said Benteen. "I won't have you sneaking around setting traps on my place."

"I told you," the deputy said. "You can't stop me. Look: I know he's taken stuff from here in the past. I know what he does with it. I know what he's going after next. I don't know when. I'm coming here and I'm waiting for him to move. If you want to see a court order, I can have one for you this afternoon. You like it or not, I'll be here. I'd just as soon you cooperated, but either way I'll be here waiting for him when he makes his move."

Benteen looked at him. "Get out of here," he said. "Go on, get off my place."

"If you're going, why are you here now?"

"I'm going tomorrow."

"You going to tell Garrett where you were tonight? You going to tell him what you were doing tonight?"

"What do you care?"

"Because I don't believe you're doing this, and you are. You're really going out there with him, aren't you?"

"I told you I was."

"Do you mind telling me why? I told you: he's not for you. He's old. He could be your father—shit, he could pretty well be your grandfather. Why?"

"He asked me."

"He asked you. Okay. You know why he asked you? No. You think you do, but you don't. Boomer told you he's crazy. Boomer's right. He's getting ready to hit the wall. That's why he asked you. To bring you in."

"It's nothing to me."

"It will be. He'll bring you in. I hope he's paying you extra."

"I hope so, too. I'll be working extra."

"You're right about that. You're wrong about what extra."

"Driving."

"You're the driver? You're not the driver. I'm the driver."

"Not any more. You been replaced."

"Shit. Replaced?"

"That's right. There's a new driver now. Me."

"You don't know what you're talking about. You're not the driver even if you are. You don't have any idea what you're getting into out there."

"I don't? You must think I'm deaf. Hasn't everybody been telling me what I'm getting into ever since I came?"

"No. They haven't. They've been telling you part, not all."

"You tell me, then."

"I've been trying. You don't get it."

"I guess I don't. Anyway, what do you care? You'll be gone, right? You can't wait to get out of here. Your big deal will get done, you'll have all that money, and you'll be gone."

"You don't know anything about that. Nothing."

"Nothing? You told me."

"No, I didn't. I didn't tell you nothing. You didn't hear anything about it. You didn't."

"Wait a minute. Is this about him? Your deals, your friends. Has that got to do with him? With that thing the other week? That wagon?"

"It's got nothing to do with anything. It's something else."

"What else?"

"Nothing. Listen, go on. You're going, go on. Go on out there. You want to be the new driver? Fine. Go ahead. Take the Benz. Take the keys. Just keep the engine running, you know? Keep that engine fucking running so when you have to split. My advice, okay? But forget about the other. My business? Forget it. It's like you said, in a week I'll be gone. You owe me that much."

"I do? For what?"

"We've been friends."

"You said that before. Is that what you call it?"

"Sure. Why not?"

"You know, Boomer? Boomer says you'll never make it. He says you'll never get out, you'll just talk about it."

"Well, Boomer can go fuck himself. He's wrong."

"Is he?"

"Yes, he is. I'm going. I got my ticket."

The glass of the windowpane was a little wavy and so as Vergil looked through it at Hugh stacking firewood in the shed, Hugh seemed wavy too, warped or misshapen, monstrous. Vergil believed it was the glass that did that and not his eyes, because if he moved his head a little and looked through the next pane, Hugh straightened out some. Still, his eyes weren't up to much; past the yard everything was, not fuzzy, but dark, as though a shadow fell there in bright day. He could see the yard well enough, and the lane, but even in the house, in his own kitchen, it sometimes got so dark in the corners and through the door that led to the stairs. It came of Vergil's eyes giving out along with the rest of him: no help for it. It came of getting to be so god damned old.

Who would have thought to get so god damned old? Though they all lived forever, all the Percys. Vergil's grandfather born in 1792; his father having had one of his hands shot off by a southern cracker of General Lee's; Vergil born when that hero was past sixty. They took each of them to himself a lifetime and a half, two lifetimes. They needed them, it seemed.

But who would have guessed all those years and years to be ahead when Vergil was, say, that kid's age? Of course, if you're that kid, you don't think you're ever going to die, but neither do you think you're going to live, or anyway not live so god damned long. You never think how you're going to go on and on. Everybody he knew had been dead for thirty years.

That kid had no idea of piling wood. Vergil watched him from the window. That kid would toss the sticks together in a kind of stack, but when the stack got high it would fall down. He'd do better to throw them in anyhow. That was the way Vergil had done it—not stacked the wood at all but just made a heap in the shed. It all burned, no matter how you kept it. There were stackers and pilers, you could take your choice. It had been good to have one job around a place that didn't have to be done right.

That kid might have something. He might have something on him. In France a lot of the boys carried a clasp knife or even a belt knife because they handled rope. Vergil had had one too. They had put him to work with the horses. The French had no idea of horses any more than they had of anything else: their men little and dark and the women not up to much. There must have been good-looking women over there someplace but Vergil never saw them; he expected they kept them locked up. Any you saw were old and low-built. Their country the same: flat country, nothing to it, and all of it ruined forever, dug up by the guns, what little timber you saw smashed, houses knocked down, whole towns knocked down. Yes, whole towns. Knocked flat, they looked like brick yards. They passed through them staring. If it had been Vergil, he said, he might have let the boches have the place rather than this happen, and a lot of the other country boys like him had said the same.

If that kid had something, a knife, even a little one, or could get one, get one of them she kept, well, then.

Vergil began rapping on the windowpane. It was loose and it rattled. He quit rapping. He didn't want to start them up, get them pouring out of the woods again, get them circling around, shrieking and carrying on the way they did. He rapped more softly so as not to bring them in. Still, the kid at the woodpile either couldn't hear him or didn't care to look around. Vergil went on rapping on the glass. He was a good-looking boy, big and straight. They would all bathe together in one of their slack, slow rivers, and those old brown Frenchwomen would come down to the bank for water and pay them no mind at all. The bolder boys would call things to the Frenchwomen, but the women paid them no mind at all. Vergil went on rapping.

You don't like how I do my work, I told him, then fire me. Go ahead. Fucking fire me.

And him just standing there, like, *Whaaa?*

That's right, fire me. Let me go. Let my people go.

No chance. Humph, he says. Humph. You just get it done. Don't have to like it, just have to do it. Humph.

Fuck you.

Course he can't fire me, can't fire anybody. Why? Because you can only fire, like, employees, and he don't want employees, he wants, what? Slaves. Or no: not slaves but soliders. You can't fire a soldier.

If she's right and I'm not driving him any more that's fine with me, too. I don't have to sit there and listen to his shit. She'll find out. She's making a mistake, that's all. She's going out there because she thinks he's her best shot. She thinks

Garrett's her way up. Plus, Hulon. She thinks he'll take care of her when Hulon comes calling. Maybe he will. But there's a price. She don't know the price. I told her: he don't need a girlfriend, he needs a keeper. You want to be his keeper? You want to be his nurse?

No.

No, and if she says fucking Boomer says I'll never get out of here, well, Boomer ain't exactly the one to talk, is he? Goes out to Texas to Fort Ratshit off in the desert, sits in the kitchen mixing up instant mashed potatoes for three years, comes right back here and sits in the kitchen at the inn doing the same thing. What a gambler, right? What an adventurer. A regular Columbus. He's talking about me never getting out? Well, he's wrong. He'll be wrong about that, won't he?

I've got to say I'm going to miss that car. That is a nice rig. Oh, nice. Seventy-five thousand bucks on four wheels and you can feel every nickel and dime of it the first time you turn the key. Nice. Well, no more. Boo-hoo. Fired at last, it looks like, anyhow part way. Just humping hay, humping wood. No more righteous rigs.

Maybe when I get my business done I'll hire her back. Outbid the old fucker. 'Till then, no Debbie Does Dallas, no Benz, nothing but expectations. Nothing but plans. Major plans.

I believe I'll write a little song:

> *Ain't got no gal.*
> *Ain't got no Benz.*
> *Don't give a shit.*
> *'Cause I got plans.*

Do you like that? I like that. I like it a lot. Which way to Nashville?

PART III

Penelope?

Penelope Bluebonnet? Are you there, Penny?

Penelope Tyler Bluebonnet?

Are you there, Bluebonnet? Are you there?

There you are. What a trip. What a trip you made. And all alone, a little gal from Gun Barrel County all by herself in the big world. Penny Bluebonnet, on the road. Were you scared? You were, weren't you, without your old Daddy by? A thousand miles. Better. Foundered your car, too, didn't you? They had to shoot it. What a ride, yes. Yes, indeed.

How about those big highways. Bluebonnet? Get on them, it's all in the endurance, isn't it, like the geese, the swans flying north. They bore along, mile after mile, day after day. Some don't make it, but none gets lost. The way is plain enough.

Let's see, you'd go 30 to Little Rock, up there, then it looks like 40 clear to Virginia, nearly. Bluebonnet, you are already way, way too far north, but do you turn around? No, you get 81 right up the mountains all the way to Pennsylvania, into New York, working north now: 88 to Albany. Hate to let you down, Bluebonnet, but you'll never see the ocean, never even smell it. Bang a right at Albany, you're in New England, Bluebonnet, you're nearly done. You pick up 91 going north like a compass needle, now, with the hills coming up in front of you, and the highway sighing under your wheels like the surf on the Atlantic shore you never saw and those big green highway signs passing grandly overhead. A long, long trip. And if that woman up there laughed at you for getting a little confused about what's New York and what's Vermont, don't you pay her any mind, Bluebonnet. For really and truly and for a fact, when you get down to it, between the two Gun Barrel County don't allow there's a damn lot to choose: one's cold, one's colder. What's the difference?

You made it, little girl. The whole country or a good piece of it passed under you: cattle land, grassland, river land, mountain land, cities, towns you raised, overtook, left behind 'til you fetched up—where? Why, right there among their little valleys, their peaceable hills, their rocky, worthless pastures. Glacier land, Bluebonnet, and being truthful with you, your poor Daddy can't see that much was gained when the glacier decided not to hang onto it. You can't get a real bowl of chili, you can't see a derrick, an elevator, a JESUS IS LORD on somebody's barn, a beef animal. They got no horizon there. That's it: you can't see the sky.

So, Bluebonnet, what are you doing up there?

* * *

"You're in here," said Mr. Benteen. "This is your room."

"Where's yours?" Tyler asked him.

"Mine? I'm downstairs. Don't you remember from when you and Cordie were out here?"

"I remember," Tyler said. "I thought you might have changed rooms."

"No," said Benteen. "You'll be all right here. You're on the quiet side. Marv and them get started pretty early, but over here they won't bother you."

"They?"

"Marv and them," said Benteen. "Wonder Boy."

"Who else?" Tyler asked.

"Well, a couple of others," Benteen said. "This is haying. Marv gets a couple more in when he needs them. I don't know: LeRoy, Gordon, maybe Henry."

"That's four or five men," Tyler said. "All them to make hay?"

"You can't waste time," Benteen said. "You got to get it done before the weather changes."

"So, four, five men in all. All working for you."

"That's right."

"All working on your hay."

"That's right," said Benteen. "How do you like it?"

"How do I like what?" Tyler asked.

"The room," Benteen said. "Your room."

"It's nice," Tyler said. "One thing, though, I want a door I can lock. This door you can't lock."

"None of the doors has got a lock," Benteen said. "I won't have it."

"Well," said Tyler, "I wish it had a lock. I'd feel a lot better if I could lock my door. You know, if I wanted to."

"Are you locking in?" Benteen asked her. "Or are you locking out?"

"Locking out."

"Who?"

"Anybody," said Tyler. "Anybody I want to."

Benteen laughed.

"You've been talking to Cordie," he said. "Cordie thinks I'm a big whoremaster out here. Don't believe all you hear. You don't need to lock your door against me."

"What about the other four?" Tyler asked.

"Them, either," said Benteen. "They do what I tell them."

"They do, huh?" Tyler asked. "Always?"

"Every time," said Benteen.

"Right," Tyler said. "Maybe they do. But Hulon doesn't know that. Does he? He's not one of yours, is he?"

"Him again," said Benteen.

* * *

And a whole new name, too: Tyler McClellan. No more Penny Bluebonnet, but sturdy Tyler, strong, straight, self-reliant traveler. Nobody's victim, nobody's fool, nobody's daughter.

Will they go for it? Not down here, Bluebonnet. Not down here, they won't. Tyler McClellan from Vermont? They'll say: *Vermont? You sure don't sound like no Vermont. Hell fire, gal, where you from?*

But then, you won't be coming back, will you, Bluebonnet? You won't be trying out your new name down here. "Tyler." Sorry, but your poor Daddy can't make his tongue form Tyler, not as a given name. Tyler: what kind of name is that for a gal, anyway? No kind. It comes to this: it's not a gal's name at all, is it, Bluebonnet? It's a man's. Like you put on men's clothing and joined the army, or like you were one of William Shakespeare's gals he wrote about (didn't he?) who dressed up like a boy and had adventures.

Damn, Bluebonnet. Look at you: new name, new place, new predicament. Or is it? Is it a new one, Bluebonnet? I mean, is it a new one, Tyler? Sorry, your old Daddy still can't say it. Tyler may fly up north, but to your Dad you remain Penny Bluebonnet, Penny T, Penny Blue. A loved child has many names.

Well, good luck, little girl, in your new place with your new name and your maybe new predicament. You'll need it. They'll freeze you up there, Bluebonnet. They'll chill you. It's not like home. They're cold. What's up there for you? I'd like to know. Whatever it is, you're into it now. You can be anything you want to be, Bluebonnet, even up there. Stay on your toes. Keep your balance, you got to be able to punch off either foot. Keep bobbing. Above all, keep your story straight.

Oh, and come to that: a nice touch. Hulon? Hulon Bear? The rattlesnakes? It's good, it's good. Top marks, Bluebonnet. Your Daddy's proud, proud. Your Daddy taught you and you learned. If you need a lie, first make sure you know what's true. Get it all right. Then change one thing.

I'm just as glad, I guess. I don't mind not having them sneaking around upstairs every night. I don't mind not having to worry about who I'll find doing what to who if I get home half an hour early. I told him the same thing. Look at it this way, I said: you can get caught up on your sleep.

You want it give it a rest, now, okay? he said. Real crabby.

I don't know, though. Right away, I'd wondered about their babies, what they'd look like. Silly, I know, but I did. Well, any mother would. With his nice blue eyes and hers brown. They say brown comes out, but Daddy had brown eyes and here are mine blue like his. Any mother would wonder, like when he was going with Ginger, in high school, I'd wonder about theirs, her with all that red hair.

Were Daddy's eyes brown? Yes. Sure they were.

Listen, I said, let Garrett have her, he wants her. She'll find out quick enough what she's into out there. If she can hack it, good luck to her. If she can't, well, she'll be back.

She won't be back, he said.

He's right about that, I expect. But she's going to have her eyes opened out there sooner or later. Garrett's restless. You can see it. He's shaky. She'll see. Not that there's any real harm to him. Not that there ever has been. That horsewoman of his, years back, that English girl, the Queen, what was it she said? Bally, some word like that.

He's quite bally, isn't he? she said.

Is he? I said. What makes you think so?

Well, I mean to say, it's plain enough, isn't it?

I don't know. Why ask me?

Well, you're all his friends and neighbors, aren't you? Perhaps you're all bally. Praps, she said: Praps you're all bally.

Perhaps we are.

Well, someone might have told me, mightn't they? she said. I mean to say, I nearly married him.

Garrett would run the women through out there like it was some kind of talent show: you couldn't keep track. What is it about him that women are taken with? Were. Well, course, he's got money, but a lot of people have got money, especially if you're from away and all his girls were, are. What else? He never was much to look at, though he's still got plenty of hair and he don't run to fat, give him that. But now he's starting to show a hard-used look. And then, he's always dressed about like a tramp. He thinks he owns this whole town and so he don't have to care how he looks. He's got a kind of arrogance, but the fact is he's not the smartest person in the world.

Does she think Garrett and Marv and them will help her if her boyfriend shows up? Protect her? Maybe. Maybe so. There's no lack of men out there. That's another thing I don't mind: her boyfriend won't be knocking on my door. I don't mind that at all. Listen, I said to him, it's for the best. Play you some checkers?

He said a word.

In the timber above top-of-the-woods, well back in there, Marvin found a place where a little oak tree grew beside an old stone wall. He cleared the dead leaves away from the space between the tree and the wall. He took out of the wall two flat stones for a seat and placed them one on top of the other at the foot of the tree. He found a heavy dead branch and laid it along the top of the wall. Then he sat on the stones with his back against the tree and rested Mr. Benteen's rifle on the branch so he could turn its barrel to cover the woods in front of him. He waited. He had left his dog at home: no dogs on a sitting hunt.

Benteen hadn't wanted to let him have the rifle. I don't even know if it'll shoot, he'd said. I don't even know if we got any shells for it any more. Benteen set some store by that rifle, though it looked like nothing but a shotgun cut down. Garrett's father had been on a hunt to Africa and he'd bought it for whatever they had out there: buffalos, rhinos. Now Garrett kept it in his book room. It ain't at all accurate, he'd told Marvin. You'll never get close enough.

Then I won't shoot, Marvin had said.

In the end, Benteen had dug around and found a box of the shells. They looked like little brass railroad flares. Be careful, Benteen said. He meant the gun. Be careful of my gun.

Marvin took the rifle back to his place. It was double barreled and it broke open like a shotgun. Marvin loaded one, raised it, cocked it, and let it go. The kick knocked him two steps back and made his shoulder go dead. He'd set up a chunk of firewood beside his house in the long grass where he kept things. An oak chunk better than six inches thick. He found the shot had gone clean through it, then gone on right in one side and out the other of an old iron stove beyond it and still had had enough left to go slap through a two-by-four that helped hold up the stove.

Look at that, said Marvin.

Marvin cleaned the barrel out. The next evening he went into the woods.

Marvin waited at his wall stand. Deer would be moving downhill pretty soon. If this big guy was still with the deer, he'd be along. How close would he have to be? Marvin had no more than forty feet between where he sat and a pine thicket, and some of that distance was in small hardwoods. He thought if he had a shot this side of the pines he could take it.

If it don't get too dark, said Marvin.

The late afternoon light was in the tops of the trees and between the trees. At his left a bird was busy on a branch, a little gray bird. It landed on the branch, which hung out over the wall in the open, and began to twitter and sing, dancing around. Then it stopped and was perfectly still. Then it dropped down into a little fir and hid there. Then, making no sound, it darted along the wall to a dead stub where it disappeared into a hole. In a minute it emerged from the hole, went to the fir, and flew off, presently to return to the exposed branch, carry on as before, and then again creep to its nest. Marvin watched the bird do that for six or seven trips: a little thing with a brain probably no bigger than the end of a pencil but smart enough to know a trick like that.

Ahead of him in the thicket a squirrel was chattering. The sun where it came down into the pines was yellow and full of dust. Marvin sat against his tree, the gun pointing out in front of him, the birds conducting their lives, their stratagems, all around him, the squirrels doing the same, the warm, slanted light coming down in dusty curtains.

Marvin sat on Mr. Benteen's tractor, mowing the top piece, except that he was about ten years old and they didn't yet use a tractor for mowing in those days, they still used horses then, so it was all wrong from the start. Benteen was walking past him through the grass, with him was Cordelia's father, Clay. Come on, they said, we're going fishing, except that there was noplace around there to fish and they carried no poles. Come on with us, Benteen and Cordelia's father said, and Marvin might have wanted to but he couldn't because there in the grass by the tractor was Cordelia's husband, and Marvin was certain he was dead, and he didn't feel he could get up and go fishing and leave him there. I can't, he seemed to say, I got to take care of him. Wait for me. But Benteen and Clay only waved and went on.

Marvin became aware that his eyes were closed. He opened them. It was nearly dark. The bird was gone and the pine thicket was quiet. It had become cool. Marvin stood up, brushed his pants down, and looked out at the woods on the other side of the wall. A whole company of moose could have gone by there at a gallop along with a brass band and he wouldn't have known it. Now he'd have to hurry to clear out of the woods before full dark. It's tough to get up at four and be a farmer and then take down your gun at the other end of that long a day and be a hunter. When Marvin broke open Benteen's rifle to unload it before starting back, he found he'd never loaded it in the first place.

It looks like you shut me out this time, Marvin said. Moose one, people nothing, it looks like.

Course it wasn't more than a day or two before Clementine Tavistock, Boomer's mom, happened to come in when I was working. Just happened to come in. And, she is tingling. Tingling. She is buzzing. If she were a dog her tongue would be like to drag on the ground. Some people ought to have their ears cut off.

Well, Clemmie said. Well, Tommy says you're short a roomer at your place.

Is that what he says? I said.

Says she's, uh, staying out at Garrett's now.

He does?

Tommy thinks she's the nicest girl, really, Clemmie says. Maybe a little mixed up.

Boomer says she's mixed up? Boomer? I didn't say anything.

I don't know how smart she is to get mixed up with Garrett, though, she says. Tommy thinks he must be drinking again. Is he drinking again?

I shut up. With Clemmie it's more fun not to give her what she wants right away. But really. Here's Boomer telling her about somebody else drinking? Boomer's no prize. If the army don't want you you've got to be pretty poor and here comes Boomer home messed up on about every kind of dope they've got. And when he gets more or less sober all he does is sleep for six months and then when he wakes up, what's he going to do? A long-haired, overweight, under-educated ex-dope fiend with a mental discharge who don't know how to do, really, anything at all. Her little Tommy.

Well, who takes him on? Who gives him a job? Who gives him a room so he can finally, Lord, get out of Clemmie's house? That's right.

He talked to Garrett, found him at the inn. I was there. Garrett asked him, Well, what did you do in the service?

Worked in the kitchen, Boomer said. I'm surprised he could remember.

Doing what? Garrett asked.

Uh, this and that.

I guess that makes you a cook, don't it? Garrett said.

I guess, Boomer said. Sure.

Sure, Garrett said. All right, then. You're a cook.

That was Boomer, and now Boomer decides Garrett's drinking? Garrett's not doing too well, Boomer figures? Garrett's making a mistake?

I don't know why Garrett can't shape up, Clemmie says. Moving a young girl in with him out there. I mean really. I don't know why he can't act his age, you know? He could be her father.

He could be her grandfather, I said. Give her a taste.

That's right, Clemmie said. That's what I mean.

And then, she says, Tommy says she'd got this other man who's following her. He's out of jail or he will be and he's looking for her. Garrett takes her on, with him? He's not thinking. What's Garrett going to do if he turns up?

Reason with him? I said. Hah.

It's not funny, Clemmie said. What if that girl was your daughter? Would you want her living out there with Garrett?

No.

I always liked Garrett, Clemmie says. How's he seem to you? How's he look to you? Tommy says he's more and more peculiar.

Peculiar. Peculiar? Least Garrett has his hair cut, don't wear a ponytail like some. I shut up.

Tommy says Hugh's not driving him any more, Clemmie said. Says he and Hugh had some kind of a bust-up out at Percys'.

Well, that's enough of that.

I know how busy you are, I said. Don't let me keep you.

Penelope Tyler McClellan: Wild Bill McClellan's girl, Shakespearean virgin, not your ordinary waif, but not un-waiflike in her way; her mother, the former Jeannette Tyler of Dallas, having parted from her father when the girl was an infant to marry, no kidding, an Italian count. She lived in Rome. Father and daughter, then, became of necessity something that looked like comrades. They became pals. It might have been fun, it was fun much of the time, for Wild Bill, careless, fond, was big and broad, the kind of cowboy entrepreneur they have down there who thinks making a lot of money, losing it, making more, is what everybody does and that it ought to be fun.

He was in and out of a hundred things before she was grown: oil and gas, airlines, resorts, shopping centers, oil and gas again, drive-in movie theaters, car dealers, restaurants. For Penelope, nothing was too big, too good. Nothing cost too much. Do pals do that? Do comrades? This one did. Wild Bill did.

One day when Penelope was seven or eight she told her father she wanted a kitten. Wild Bill went out to buy her one. He came back with a pony. He hadn't been able to find a kitty, he said, but how about this? Penelope would ride her pony around the golf course beside which they then lived, with Wild Bill following in an electric golf cart. He kept his eye on her, she must be safe on her pony. And if golfers objected—well, they didn't. Wild Bill damn well owned the golf course and whoever didn't want to share it with Wild Bill's little gal and her pony could go play on somebody else's damn course.

* * *

"No," said Mr. Benteen. "I don't blame you for running away from him, if he's what you say."

"He's worse," Tyler said. "He's a killer. He would have killed me."

"All right," said Benteen. "Sure, you ran. What else could you do? The police won't take care of you."

"They won't even try," Tyler said.

"What I don't see," Benteen said, "is why you couldn't get some help down there. Don't you have any friends, family? Don't you have a brother, a father? Somebody to take care of him for you?"

"I don't have any brothers," Tyler said.

"You got a father," said Benteen. "Everybody does. What about him?"

"He can't help."

"Why not?" Benteen asked her. "Is he too old? Is he as old as me?"

"Nobody's that old," said Tyler.

"Well, it don't matter," said Benteen. "You did the best thing. You ran. You ran up here. Now you're out of it. Forget it."

"Are you telling me to forget Hulon?"

"I am."

"That's what that boy said."

"He was right," said Benteen.

"He was wrong," said Tyler. "He was so wrong. You are both so wrong. You don't know. Hulon will not just let me go because I've gone. He will not. He will come up here and try to take me back. Or worse."

"No, he won't," said Benteen.

"Why not?"

"I told you," Benteen said. "You lost him. When you came up here, you lost him."

"You think so," said Tyler.

"All right," said Benteen. "Look: I'll tell you. You're here.

You're on my place now. If he comes to my place, I'll take care of him. That was what we said, wasn't it? On my place I can take care of him. I can take care of you."

"On your place, you're the boss," Tyler said.

"I am," said Benteen.

"So what about the people who stole your cart?" Tyler asked. "What about the other things you've had stolen? People come on your place and rob you all the time and you don't even know it. You can't stop them. What's to stop Hulon, then, if you can't stop the others?"

"They're different," said Mr. Benteen.

* * *

That old boy has never been in Texas, Bluebonnet. You take it from your old Dad. That business about the Llano? The rattlers? The Mexicans? No, Bluebonnet.

No. Now, understand me: he didn't make it all up. It happened to somebody, all right, but it didn't happen to him. Get it right, then change one thing. We're not the only ones who know that trick. That old boy's deep.

How do I know? Hell, Bluebonnet, don't ask me that. Everybody's been telling you that old boy has not got all six chambers loaded. Anybody can tell he's never been out of those damn old hills of his. He'd be scared to, and he'd be right. The fact is, they're all played out up there, Bluebonnet. The last live fellow left a hundred years ago and the next live fellow hasn't come yet. Any that stay behind, there's something wrong with them. You can be anything you want to be, Bluebonnet, but they don't know that. That old boy wouldn't last a day down here. Here there's no rules, up there there's nothing but. Nothing but rules, Bluebonnet. Rules, limits. They can't do without them. He wouldn't last a day down here, not an hour. Why? Because of the sky. It's the sky, Bluebonnet: those old boys up there? Their woods? Their hills? They're to keep out the sky. Those boys can't stand so much sky.

She didn't say what they were up to out there. She didn't say and was I about to ask? I got enough to think about.

Clemmie, that's Boomer's mom, says he's drinking again, I said. Is he?

No, she said. Not that I can see.

Well, I said, you'd see if he was, wouldn't you?

Maybe not, she said. I sleep upstairs, you know. My room's upstairs.

Sure, I said. Course. It's none of my business where you sleep.

He's gone most of the day as it is, she said. He's out around the place with Marvin and the men and then he goes off in the woods.

Goes off in the woods? I said. What do you mean? You mean by himself?

She said yes, by himself.

Does Marv know about that? I asked her.

I don't know, she said. He goes off over the hill to where they're cutting trees. I think he's worried they'll sneak across and cut his trees. Can they do that?

No, I said. I don't expect so.

Then, um, nighttime we sit around, you know? she said. Sit around. That's it. Sometimes we sit on the porch. We talk, oh, I don't know what about. Hulon. I tried to warn him about Hulon but he can't seem to care, he won't even lock the doors, so I gave up. He'll see. He'll find out. Rest of the time, we talk. Then I go off to bed. Ten, ten-thirty. That's it.

That's all? I said.

That's all there is, she said. Sometimes he stays up, sometimes not. Sometimes I think he stays up all night. He's talking to somebody, late. I hear him. Who's he talking to?

Just himself, I said.

Well, I hear him, she said.

You don't sleep? I asked her.

Not too good, she said.

Well, I bet she don't. I wouldn't. She's lying in her bed up there all night waiting for the show to start, you might say. Waiting for him to come in to her, not knowing when he'll come, not knowing how it will be when he does. I wouldn't sleep, either. Like you've seen the mare when they bring the stallion to her paddock, or even before he comes, knowing he's coming, how she'll be keyed up, dance around. Not that old Garrett's much of a stallion. But her lying in her bed waiting for him as though he was Man o' War.

That's it, she said. That's all. Listen, do you think he's you know?

Garrett? I said. I don't think so. No, I would have to say not. Look: you've been out there, what is it, a week?

Eight days, she said.

A week plus, I said. I was laughing. Just because the man don't break down your door the first night, I said, don't make him you know. Might be it takes him a while to get up to speed. Garrett's not young, remember. Even a little thing like you can't make him have fewer years than he's got.

You have got no right laughing at me, she said.

I'm not laughing at you, I told her. I'm laughing at him. But, no, listen: Garrett will come around. One way or another. You'll see. Be patient. Take him for what he is. He's got his own way of doing things, is all. A touch of the poet, my Daddy used to say. Old Garrett's got a touch of the poet about him.

You got no right laughing at him either, you know, she said.

Don't I? I said.

A touch of the poet, Daddy said. The lunatic, the lover, and the poet are of imagination all compact, he'd say. Compact? Wait. Couldn't be compact, could it? Compact's something else. Composed?

Well, I wouldn't know, she said. Back up on her huffy horse.

Compact. Daddy wouldn't have used a regular word. The lunatic, the lover, and the poet are of imagination all compact. That's Shakespeare. We'd all laugh. Garrett, too.

I don't think you should make fun of him, is all, she said. All you say he's done for you.

I make fun of anybody I want, I said. We got Free Speech, you know. Now, look, as far as Garrett: you see Marv, you got that? You make sure Marv knows about that business of his going out to that logging place of Condostas'. You make sure Marv knows he's doing that by himself, that he's out there by himself. Maybe it's okay. I don't know. But I don't like it.

Why not? she said.

I just don't.

Damn, Bluebonnet, did you have to go so far? Why? Isn't Texas big enough, wide enough, to put between you and . . .

you and, well, you and whatever you need something between you and? I guess not. I tried, Bluebonnet. Your Daddy tried.

No, things were not always what they ought to have been or what your Daddy tried to make them be. He knows that, Bluebonnet. But whatever was wrong, your Daddy could have fixed it. Did you have to run? Your old Dad tried to hold it all together for you, all those balls your Daddy tried to keep up in the air: the money, the home, the time, the vacations, the cars, the schools, the friends, the pets. The love. All those damn old balls, he had to keep up in the air at once, all the time, never dropping one? You can't do it, Bluebonnet, not alone.

Not alone. Friends, Bluebonnet: there is the bottom of it, the heart of it. Friends are everything. You can be anything you want to be, but to do it you got to have friends. Not for success. For survival. Business? It's all about friends, isn't it? you do things for people, they do things for you. You take care of people, they take care of you. Real simple. In business, it comes through money, or selling, or whatever it is, but it's based on friends—a kind of friends. Loving? The same: you care, you get cared for; you provide, you get provided for. It's based on friends. You make the world your friends, Bluebonnet—and you know I don't mean in any damn Hallmark card way—but you make this world your friends because that's the only way to get by.

And that, Bluebonnet, is why your Daddy doesn't know about your old boy up there. Your poor Dad has got a problem with him. Not because he's an old man who likes a young woman around—there's plenty of better men than him who have liked that. Not because he likes a drink: your old Daddy wouldn't wish you on a teetotaler, Lord no. Not even because he comes unstuck and jumps his fence from time to time. Not because of any of those things, Bluebonnet, but because he's got no friends.

"Daddy, Daddy, Daddy," Tyler said. "That's all you get with her, over and over. Her Daddy said this. Her Daddy said that."

"Well," said Mr. Benteen, "she misses him."

"Her Daddy this, her Daddy that. What her Daddy used to say."

"She misses him," said Benteen. "That's why. Cordie hasn't had much luck with men, it looks like. Her husband dying so young. Clay never around much, at least not 'til toward the end. Now Wonder Boy."

"Clay?"

"Clay, her father," Benteen said. "Clay. He wasn't much of a father, I don't guess, come to that."

"He wasn't?" Tyler asked.

"Not much, I guess," Benteen said. "Clay was restless and Clay was smart. He went into the war, then he got into newspapering. There's none of that here. Clay came and went. That was him that was in Texas. What I told you, with the snakes? That was Clay, his story. Not mine. He was down there, not me. Clay was all over the world: South America, Africa, I don't know where."

"I thought he was a schoolteacher," said Tyler.

"That was later," said Benteen.

"Why did you say it was you that was in Texas?" Tyler asked.

"I don't know," Benteen said. "Maybe I thought a man as much older than you as I am had best seem as though he had been around and knew something."

"You've been around."

"No," said Benteen. "Not any at all."

"That's not what I heard."

"I know what you heard," said Benteen. "Around here,

yes. Around here, I have been. But that's all. And then, too, with Clay: Clay and I were kids together, boys together here, all our life. So, with Clay, if it happened to him—Texas, say—in a way it happened to me. If he did it, I did it. I thought."

"I get it," Tyler said.

Benteen laughed at her.

"No, you don't," he said. "How could you? There's nothing to get. The thing was, Clay took off, and I stuck it out here. Course, I had this place, you see. I had to keep up the place. It's a big place and even if it ain't much of a farm any more it takes a good deal of running. My father let it go to hell. He was gone a lot, more like Clay. Not smart like Clay, though. None of the Benteens has ever been real bright."

"Why not?" Tyler said. "You went through school, didn't you?"

"I did," Benteen said.

"You went to college?"

"Not much," said Benteen. "I passed in and out of college pretty quick."

"Like that boy," said Tyler.

"Not like him," said Benteen. "Not that quick. See, in my time you could quit and go to the war. In fact, you were meant to."

"What war? World War II?"

"That was the one," Benteen said.

"You fought in World War II?"

"Well, I wouldn't say fought," Benteen said. "Chairborne, I was. Glad of it, too. That fighting, that's no joke, you know. You can get killed."

"Did what's his name? Her father?"

"Clay."

"Did he fight?"

"He did," said Benteen. "Anway, if Cordie goes on a little

bit about her Daddy, it's because she misses him. I miss him, myself."

"Will you tell me something straight out?" Tyler asked him.

"I don't know," Benteen said. "I'll tell you what I can."

"What am I doing here?"

"What are you doing?" said Benteen. "Hiding. Hiding, aren't you? Hiding from that fellow you're so scared of? That snake fellow?"

"I mean for you," Tyler said. "What am I doing for you?"

"Driving," said Benteen. "You're the driver. Aren't you?"

"Is that all? I mean, I'm here. I wait. Nothing happens."

"What do you think ought to happen?" Benteen asked her.

"Something," Tyler said.

"No," Benteen said. "You don't see it yet. You came. You're here. It ain't quite what you thought. You say nothing happens? Well, that's the kind of place this is. Clay, you know, when he came back here toward the end, he was sick and broke down, needed it quiet. Thought he'd teach school. Thought he'd write the town history. He always had to be writing something, thought he'd work on the town history. So he went to the library, the town hall, got the old records, deeds, maps. Read it all up. Writing the town history, you see? But he had to quit. He had to give it up. Why? Because he found out there wasn't anything to write. Nothing ever happened here. The history of the town is that the town has no history, Clay said. He said, I give it up."

"Well," Tyler said, "that's not exactly what I meant."

"Yes, it is," said Benteen.

"I thought you were going to tell me straight," said Tyler. "All I get is another thing her Daddy said. I mean, now you're doing it too, aren't you?"

"I guess I am," said Benteen. "It's all I know to tell you."

"Daddy, Daddy, Daddy, all over again," Tyler said.

She raised her arms high over her head and stretched herself in her chair.

"Daddy, Daddy, Daddy," Tyler said. "Let me tell you about my Daddy sometime."

"Go ahead," said Benteen.

"No," Tyler said. "No chance."

Never what you could call a bad-tempered boy. Moody, sometimes, sure, but not bad tempered until now. Now you can't kid him along at all, can't get him answering you back, showing how smart he thinks he is. If you touch him now, he snaps like a rat trap.

I wish you'd sweeten up, I told him. I'm not the one that took your girlfriend. I don't know why you're biting me.

You think I give a *blank* about that? he said, and he knows I won't stand for that. I told him.

Look, I told you, you use that language in my house, you can go live down at the dump with the rest of the garbage. I won't hear that word said. Do you understand me?

Okay, he said. All right.

If it's not her then what is it? I said.

Nothing, he said.

Well, I said, if it's nothing then I wish you'd sweeten up. He drank his coffee.

Know who I saw yesterday? I asked him.

No.

Ginger, I said.

Is that right? he said.

She's working at the Chevy place in Brattleboro, I said. Goes down every day. She's living here at home.

I'll bet she is, he said.

What does that mean?

Nothing.

That's all he'd say about her. But Ginger's all right. She's solid. And doing very well. She started down there just answering the phone but now she's getting into selling. Women buy cars too and a lot of them would rather buy a car from another woman. Somebody finally figured that out. Ginger's doing very well down there.

Why don't you call her up? I said.

I don't think so, he said. That was all: I don't think so.

Then is when he said I've been thinking about taking some time off. And I thought he meant, like, a day—go to Brattleboro, White River, go to the new stores, have a good dinner, a movie. I think that's a real good idea, I said. You do that.

No, he said, I mean a long time, get out of here for a while.

I see, I said. Real calm, now. How long a while are we talking about? And he said I don't know.

Where were you thinking of going? I said. And he said, I don't know, maybe out west.

I see, I said. Real calm. Okay. All right. Well, what are you going to do out there?

I don't know, he said. Then he said he had to get to work.

That was it, then. That was when he said it, how he said it. Take some time off. What time? Don't know. Where? Don't know. What doing? Don't know. He left, and I guess I was starting to get the kitchen cleaned up before I got ready to go over to the inn when the phone rang. Not yet seven in the morning, I jumped a foot. A man I never heard before with a loud voice and a kind of lah-de-dah way of talking, saying Is Hugh there, please? Is Hugh *they-ah*? He just left, I told him. Ah, he said.

Ah, will he be back soon, do you know?

Not 'til tonight, I said. He's working.

Ah, he said again—this real kind of snob voice: *Ah, Ah*—and I thought, Who is this?

Ah, he said, well, perhaps you'd give him a message?

Who's this? I said.

A friend of Hugh's, the man said. My name is Guest. Would you tell him his shipment's ready? Ask him to call me. He knows the number. Would you do that?

What shipment? I said. Who is this?

If you'll simply give Hugh the message, he'll understand, he said. Many thanks. Real polite. He hung up. And I thought, well, whatever this is it's nothing good. Whatever it is I don't like it. And it's not yet seven o'clock in the morning.

Tyler found Mr. Benteen in his office in the barn. He sat at his desk in there, looking. He was looking at the window behind the desk, where the sun lit the dust and cobwebs that covered the little panes of dirty glass. That was a window in a barn, not one in a house. Nobody had ever washed it. A hundred years of dirt. Dirt that old isn't dirt.

"Boomer's here," Tyler said. "He wants to see you."

"Who?" Benteen said.

"Boomer. He's here to see you, he says."

"Where?"

"Here," Tyler said. "He's right out here. I said. Are you okay?"

"What does he want?" Benteen asked.

"I don't know," Tyler said. "He wants you."

"All right," said Benteen.

Boomer stood in the doorway with Tyler waiting behind him. He came into the office.

"How are you doing?" Boomer asked Benteen.

"Good," said Benteen. "You?"

"Good," said Boomer. "Well, you know."

"What do you want?" Benteen asked.

"Well," said Boomer. "I'd like it better if we could talk alone, if you don't mind."

"I don't mind," Tyler said. She turned to leave the office.

"Stay where you are," Benteen said. "Sit."

He looked at the corner of his desk. Tyler passed behind Boomer where he stood in front of Benteen's desk. She sat on the corner of the desk.

"What do you want?" Benteen asked Boomer again.

Boomer sighed.

"Listen," he said. "I don't mind her except I wouldn't want Cordie to know I was out here. You know?"

"Why not?" Benteen asked.

"Um, well, it's about Hugh, is why," said Boomer. "That's the reason."

Benteen didn't say anything. After a moment, Tyler looked around at him but still he didn't say anything.

"What about him?" Tyler asked Boomer.

"Look," said Boomer. "I don't like this, you know? I don't like coming out here with this. But I didn't feel like it was right not to, so I did. I'm here, so I'm going to lay it out for you, just lay it out."

"Do it, then," Tyler said, but Benteen sat and watched Boomer and didn't speak or change unless it was around his eyes which drew back into his head a little, seemed to, or turned a little darker color, as when a high cloud passes over water.

"Do it, then," Tyler was saying.

"He's stealing from you, okay?" Boomer said. "He has

153

been and he is. I can't prove it, but it's true. It was him took your cart that got wrecked there the other week. It was Hugh that did that—or, not him all by himself but he was a part of it. He's robbing you. That's it."

Tyler turned to Benteen. His face was as though a heavy glass visor had fallen into place in front of it; you could see him through it, but his face was behind it now. What was he doing? He was looking around to either side like a man who has dropped something on the floor. In the corner behind his desk was a barrel where they kept spare tool handles: axe handles, pick handles, scythe handles, and the like.

"I thought you had a right to know," said Boomer. "That's all. I thought I had a duty, you know, to tell you what I know—what I knew."

"Damn you," Benteen said to him. "Damn you, you're nothing but a god damned spy, are you. A spy." He stood up quickly, pitching his chair over behind him, and pulled an axe handle out of the barrel.

"Wait a minute," said Boomer, but before any of them knew what he was doing, Benteen had come around the desk and swung the axe handle sidearm like a tennis racket. Boomer stepped back and the handle missed him, but Benteen brought it right around the other way backhanded and this time he got Boomer on the right shoulder.

"What?" said Boomer. "Wait. Ow. Jesus."

"Come in here to me and sell out your friend," said Benteen. He hit Boomer in the side hard enough to make him stumble, and he was bringing the axe handle back again when Tyler got him in her arms from behind and held on. Benteen was off balance, and he and Tyler fell to the floor alongside the desk with her underneath him holding on to him around his body and their legs in the air.

"That's enough," said Tyler. They lay together on the floor with Boomer on his feet rubbing his shoulder.

"Jesus, Garrett," said Boomer.

"Get out of here, Boomer," said Tyler. She had rolled out from under Benteen, who was on his hands and knees on the floor like an animal.

"Let me help you," Boomer said, and he came toward Benteen to help him up.

"I've got him," said Tyler. "Go ahead, now."

"What could I do, you know?" Boomer asked her. "Knowing that, what else could I do? It was like I was stealing from him myself if I didn't say anything."

"It's all right, Boomer," Tyler said. "But go on, now. Get away from here, now. I've got him."

Boomer left.

"What's the matter with you?" Tyler said. "You hurt him."

Benteen got up off the floor onto his knees and looked around for his chair but he had upset it so he sat back on the floor and leaned against the desk. He was breathing hard.

"I hurt him?" he said. "I ought to killed him. Coming in here to me with a story like that? Like a god damned spy? That deputy stood right there and told me the same thing but with him it don't signify, you expect it."

"He thought he had to," Tyler said. "You helped him. He wanted to help you. You took care of him. He wanted to take care of you. He thought he owed you to tell you if he thought Hugh was a thief."

"There is no lack of thieves around here," said Benteen, "but he ain't one of them. Damn him."

"No," said Tyler. "Damn you. You're going down the tubes on me, here, aren't you? That's what this is. They were right. You're going around the bend on me, here."

"Are you hurt?" Benteen asked her. "Did you get hurt when we went over? You got a grip on you, you know that?"

"I'm okay."

"Where's Marvin?" Benteen asked her.

"I don't know," said Tyler. "Mowing? He could be any-where."

"Get Marvin," said Benteen. "I need him."

Ginger Browning. She saw Ginger. Why don't I call Ginger?

I don't think so.

I don't think so. You take on Ginger and you might as well lock a chain to one ankle and hook the other end on a mountain. You are here. Ginger's a lifer.

I'd ask her. We were going out, and I'd ask her, Don't you ever want to leave?

No.

Don't you ever want to go anywhere? Travel?

No.

Don't you ever want to see new people, have new friends?

No.

It's her mother. She can't handle not living near her mother. Her mother, get it? This ferocious old beast who can see in the dark like a fucking owl and hear even better, can like hear a zipper at about a thousand yards. Ginger wants to live near her.

She's no dope, either, I don't mean that. Working at the Chevy place, getting into selling. Ginger's smarter than all the guys at the Chevy place put together. But it don't matter. She could get to be the head of GM and she'd still have to live here with her mother down the road, have to see her every day.

I don't think so.

Yes, I see you. I see you, too. Hi, there. Hi. Wave hello. Wave hello, now. Hi. Go fuck yourself.

What do you want? Getting ready to piss yourself again, are you? Oh, yeah, boy, I wouldn't want to miss that.

Yes, hi, there. Vergil. My man. How's it hanging, there? Giving it a pretty good workout today? Good. Good to hear. Go to it. Don't mind me. I'm just here for the wood. That's right, yeah. I see you, too. Hi.

Three more days. Maybe four or five. Then, which way? Well, you pretty much have to go west, don't you? West and south. Drop down to, what is it, 80, turn on the radio, sit back, and take the ride. All alone. Boo-hoo. Goodbye.

Someday he'll figure out he's not missing stuff any more. Maybe he'll find his antique wind thing up there came out of some body shop. He'll get together with fucking Rackstraw then and they'll go, *Duhhh, I wonder where Cordie's boy is. You don't suppose . . . Duhhh*. Beautiful.

That's unless he's fucked himself to death by that time with Debbie Does Dallas. Not likely. What did I tell her? He don't need a girlfriend, he needs a keeper. Them driving around. Them sitting on the front porch all night, talking, for Christ's sake, like your fucking granny and gramps. No action I can see. I feel like walking right up to them, there, saying, *Hey, Garrett, you're not using it, can I take it for a ride?*

Well, not this time.

Good bye. Going alone, then, it's best. Though I about figured she'd come, the two of us going down the road, keeping ahead of her man back there, that freak, keeping moving. Or, no: he catches up. Somewhere in the West, in some desert, he catches up to us. Or, no: it's in some crummy, run-down motel like they got out there. We're in bed and he busts in and we have it out right there: *bam, bam.* Cut that fucker down right there, then we're back in the car, we're gone. *Zooooomm.*

It looked like us two would leave them all together here,

leave them behind, leave them exactly like they are, were, will be, like walking out of a fucking wax museum at five o'-clock: turn out the lights, lock the door.

Because her coming here to town in the first place was like a signal, like a sign that it was time to stand up, quit fooling, take what was on the table, and go. It don't matter, though. Travel alone, you get farther.

Yes, yep, there you still are, by gully. I see, you, too. Wave bye-bye. Wave bye-bye, now.

What do you want?

Marvin knew a place not far from top-of-the-woods where there was a spring. The deer went to water to that spring, and if the big fellow he was looking for was with them there might be some sign. So the day he took the baler up there he brought Mr. Benteen's rifle and after quitting time, when the bales were made and lying so neat all up and down the field waiting to be picked up, and the long shadows were reaching out from the woods across the bright, shorn mowing, he got the rifle and he and his old dog went in there for a look. He loaded the rifle this time.

At least I'll be ready for him, said Marvin. Not saying I'll get a shot, but if we find him.

They didn't find him but they found his tracks. The deer had left their delicate footprints here and there in the mud beside the spring, and sunk deep into the mud over and among the deer tracks, and circling the whole spring, were the other tracks: like the deer's, a cleft heart, but huge, the size of a saucer, and driven two, three inches down into the mud by the prodigious weight of the beast.

Look at that, Marvin said.

He was no Indian, but the tracks looked fresh to him, and he knew, he knew, that big thing was right there in the woods around the spring, but the woods were thick and it was getting dark, and though he peered and listened, he saw nothing.

Then his dog, who had been drinking at the spring, seemed to mark something in the woods. He stood alert, then made off around the water and into the trees. Marvin heard him moving off through the brush. He didn't want him in there but he didn't want to call him for fear the big fellow would hear. He put himself inside the woods just at the edge at a place where he could lay the barrel of Benteen's rifle across a pine branch. He could see the whole spring and the woods opposite. He waited there.

Might be he'll drive him this way, Marvin said.

Presently he thought he could see where the shadows in among the trees changed, grew darker, lighter, obscurely moved and passed. That was the big fellow, it had to be, and Marvin bent to his gun, shut one eye, and tried putting the sight on the spot. The shadow was surely moving toward him now, toward the spring. Marvin cocked the gun, put his finger on the trigger and the tip of his tongue between his front teeth. But all the time he could hear his dog over there moving through the woods. If the dog would come out, show himself—but even if the big fellow emerged into the clear, how could he shoot, knowing that if he hit the creature the shot might go right through it and off into the woods where his dog was?

Marvin let the hammer down, stood straight. He looked into the woods where he'd been aiming. You couldn't say for sure that there was anything moving in there, not for sure, nothing but the last light and the shadows, elements of the gathering night. No sound of the dog now.

When the dog turned up a few minutes later he came not from the spring but from behind Marvin's position, from the direction of the mowing. He'd picked up a lot of burrs on his chest, and Marvin leaned Benteen's rifle against a tree and got down on one knee to work on them.

Whose side are you on in this thing, anyway? Marvin asked the dog.

Hugh found Mr. Guest waiting in his station wagon in the turnout at the top of Diamond Mountain. Together they put the substitute ram, wrapped in paper and tape, into Hugh's car. Then Hugh and Mr. Guest sat in the station wagon.

"Who was it I spoke to?" Mr. Guest asked.

"My mom," Hugh said. "What did she say?"

"She wanted to know who was calling," said Mr. Guest.

"I'll bet she did."

It was a pretty spot up there, the highest open place for miles. The sun was nearly down. Banks of purple cloud lay along the west like shoals of ink, beneath them a band of scarlet light, livid, flaring, beneath that the unending hills now withdrawing into darkness, except for the highest of them, which took the last light: in the south, Stratton Mountain, in the north a similar peak, Killington or possibly Ascutney.

"I imagined you'd be able to work it from inside," said Mr. Guest.

"Me, too," Hugh said. "You can't. It's too built, the what do you call it, the little tower up there."

"The cupola," said Mr. Guest.

"The shutter things are nailed down, you can't open

them," said Hugh. "I'd have to take a bar and tear the whole tower apart to get the thing in there to take it out."

"Well, it's a difficulty, isn't it?" said Mr. Guest.

"No, it ain't," said Hugh. "I'll go up outside, the side away from the house. I'll have a rope tied up in the tower. Time comes, I'll go up inside, toss the rope out, go down, around, go up the rope, get the thing, go back down the rope. What do you figure the real one weighs?"

"More than ours does," said Mr. Guest.

"Okay," said Hugh. "I'll get another rope for it, lower it from the roof. So what? It's still easy."

"You forget your own rope, my boy," Mr. Guest said. "You can't leave it hanging from the cupola. No one must know you've been there. That's the whole point. There must be no sign. You'll have to lower the vane, climb down the rope outside, then go back up inside, untie the rope and drop it out. Then you'll have to clear away both ropes along with the vane before you can leave."

"Right."

Mr. Guest shook his head. He tapped his fingers on the steering wheel in front of him, shook his head again.

"I don't like it, my boy," he said. "I see it as a difficulty. You're willing, I appreciate that, but I don't like it. I like it less and less. Quite apart from my not wanting to see you discovered and, ah, embarrassed, you could be hurt. Quite apart from that, it's of little good to me to have you lying under Mr. Benteen's barn with Mr. Benteen's golden ram in your arms and your back broken."

"Nobody's back is going to get broken," Hugh said. "I've climbed ropes. I can do it."

"I think not, my boy," said Mr. Guest. "I say we stand down."

"You can stand wherever you want," said Hugh. "I'm going. I'm getting the thousand."

"If that's your concern," said Mr. Guest, "I'll give you two hundred fifty for your time to date. We'll think of something else."

"Fuck two fifty," said Hugh. "I've got the switcher, I've got the rope. I'm going ahead. If you don't want it, fuck you, too. Maybe I'll give it to Dudley Doright. How's that? I bet he'll want it."

"Well, well, let's be calm," said Mr. Guest. "You seem so bent on this project, my boy. Why? There are other objects. We'll think of something else another time."

"Wrong," said Hugh. "When this is done, I get the thousand and I go."

"Go? Go where?"

"West," said Hugh.

"You're joking," said Mr. Guest.

"No joke," said Hugh. "When this is done, I'm gone. I'm out of here."

"Why, for heaven's sake?"

"Why?" said Hugh. "Because I'm all done here, okay? There's nothing here. You want me to spend the rest of my life humping hay and ripping off weather vanes?"

"But look, my boy," said Mr. Guest.

He pointed out the window of the car toward the crimson west where the last light had nearly left the cool and quiet hills. Above them, above the mantle of clouds, serene, the evening star.

"Look at what it is you propose to leave. You've a beautiful home, a healthy outdoor life, honorable work—well, perhaps not strictly speaking, but who's harmed? Millions would give all they own to have a life here."

"They can have mine, then," Hugh said.

Mr. Guest sighed. He shook his head.

"Well, well," he said. "You bring me bad news, my boy. But perhaps, perhaps a rest isn't altogether a bad idea. It might be best to take a break."

"I'm not talking about a break," said Hugh. "I'm talking about for good. I won't be back."

162

"Won't you?" said Mr. Guest. "Don't be too sure, my boy. You're twenty-two? Twenty-three? Don't promise yourself too many things at twenty-two. It's not a very nice world. It's certainly not a beautiful world. This is not far off the best it can be. You'll find that out."

"Sure," said Hugh. "So do we do business or not?"

"In any case," Mr. Guest went on, "a break. A hiatus. A *détente* could do well. It could do well for both of us. Talking of your friend deputy Rackstraw, I had a visit from him the other day. I did, indeed. He was with a man named Kennedy, of the Massachusetts State Police. Do you know they actually came to my house? Kennedy of course I've dealt with before, many times, but your deputy Rackstraw seemed so zealous. Zeal, my boy, beware zeal. *Surtout, pas de zèle*. Who said that?"

"So do we have a deal, here?" Hugh asked him.

"By all means," said Mr. Guest. "You seem so bent, my boy. And then you ride off into the sunset, never to return? Well, well, then, we'll go forward as planned, since you wish it. Youth will be served."

"Fucking-A right it will," said Hugh.

"Talleyrand, my boy," said Mr. Guest. "Old Talleyrand said it."

What happened, Bluebonnet? Where did your Daddy drop it, where did things go wrong? Did things go wrong? Or is this just the way it always works out after all. How are you supposed to know? Damn, Bluebonnet. You only get to go through once, so how are you supposed to know?

But I go back over every little thing, and I'll tell you, Bluebonnet, it doesn't look too bad to me. Hell, no, it doesn't at all. So I can't see what happened. Sure, here and there, but altogether it wasn't so bad. Was it? And a lot of it was good—a lot of it was good. Wasn't it? How, then, did we wind up like this? I wish you'd tell me because I would like to know. I would like to know where I lost the path. I would like to know where I lost you.

The last couple of days, you know, Bluebonnet, thinking back. So much fun. That pony I got you. Western saddle, all the tack, but real little, like you were. Up you'd climb and ride all over Braemuir, cross the creek there on Nine, over the greens, me bringing up the rear in that damn old cart like I was your caddy, your footman, you riding like a princess. Those old boys would stop their play, see you riding by. They didn't really mind. *Hey, Wild Bill*, they'd call out. *Who's that gal you're chasing? Hey, Wild Bill, you reckon you can run her down by the eighteenth?* They didn't really mind. How could they mind? How could they mind you? Good times.

You can be anything you want to be, Bluebonnet. That has been your Daddy's faith. I put my faith in that and I put my faith in friends. In people. You do things for people, they will do things for you and you will be anything you want to be. Your old Daddy put his faith in people. He put his faith in you. Did he do wrong?

What was it we called him, Bluebonnet? The pony? Prince or some such damn name. Duke. Champion. I don't know. You gave him some damn name like that. Kids are so conventional, Bluebonnet. They got so little imagination.

* * *

"Look," said Benteen. "If you want to bail out, go ahead. I wouldn't blame you. Just get Marv for me."

They sat on the porch of Benteen's house, in two of Marvin's hard wooden chairs set side by side to look across the lawn to the barn.

"I'm not bailing out," said Tyler. "I can't find him. He's mowing. He's off someplace. I'll keep looking."

"Find Marv," said Benteen.

But when Tyler got up to go look for Marvin, he made her stay.

"Wait," he said. "Stay. Stay here now."

Tyler sat down again. She looked at Benteen.

"You know, Boomer could probably come back out here with that deputy and have you arrested," said Tyler. "Do you understand that?"

"Have me arrested?" said Benteen. "For what?"

"For what?" Tyler said. "For assault. You assaulted him. You know you did. You hit him with an axe handle."

"You don't know what you're talking about," said Benteen.

"I'm talking," said Tyler. "I'm talking about you beating that boy like he was a slave. What do you think you are?"

"He's no slave," said Benteen. "And he won't be back here with that deputy."

"No," said Tyler. "He won't. Maybe he'd do better if he would. Maybe you would, too. You think because you've helped them, all of them, one time and another, they owe you. They're your friends, you think. You call them and they'll come. You're wrong. That's not the way it works."

"No, it ain't," said Benteen. "They'll come, but not because they're my friends and not because they owe me."

"Why, then?"

"Because they have to."

"Why?"

"Because we got this place together here," said Benteen. "We got work to do here."

"Your work," Tyler said. "Not theirs. Your work. Your place. Not theirs. No wonder that boy can't wait to get out.

No wonder he's stealing from you—if he is. I don't know if I'd blame him if he were. Nothing's his, everything's yours."

"He won't leave," said Benteen. "If he does, he'll come back."

"I hope you're wrong," Tyler said. "What's this place got for him? Pitching hay? Digging holes? Chopping wood?"

"What's the matter with that?" said Benteen. "At least it's real work. What's he going to do away? Wait tables? Sell hamburgers? Pump gas? Be somebody's servant, is what it comes to. Pitching hay and digging holes ain't so mean."

"Your hay. Your holes. He's still a servant. He's your servant."

"He's not," said Benteen. "He belongs here. That's not being a servant. The work don't matter. It's the place."

"Well," Tyler said. "I see you've got this all figured out. I hope it makes sense to you, because it sure doesn't to me. Of course, I work waiting tables. Your tables. At your hotel. So maybe I'm not bright enough to get it."

"It's different for you," Benteen said.

"Oh, come on," said Tyler. "Oh, no. Not that. Why is it different? Because I'm a woman, right?"

"No," said Benteen "You don't listen. Cordie's a woman. It's different because this ain't your place."

"It could be," Tyler said.

"It's too late," said Benteen. "Too late. It's going so it ain't going to be anybody's place. They're coming and it's no drill. You know what I mean."

"No, I don't," Tyler said. "You mean where they're cutting trees?"

"There," said Benteen. "Other places. It's my job to stop them and I don't know how. I don't know if I can. I don't think I can. Something Marv said."

"What did he say?" Tyler asked.

"He said, If you got to buy it it don't count," said Benteen.

"What's that mean?" Tyler asked him.

Althea had gone to her sister's. She had taken off for a couple of hours while Hugh was at Vergil's house putting in his wood. She'd be back in time to get Vergil's lunch, she said; until then it wasn't likely he'd need anything.

Hugh didn't like it, but he stayed at the woodpile and paid no attention to Vergil watching him from the kitchen window—until Vergil kept rapping on the glass.

At last Hugh threw in a chunk, turned, and faced the window.

"Okay," said Hugh. "Okay, okay, okay. What do you want?"

Vergil beckoned him. Hugh went to the window, but Vergil went on beckoning and turned his head toward the door. It looked as though he wanted Hugh to go around and come into the kitchen.

"I'm not going in there," said Hugh. "I'm out here. You're in there. I like it like that."

Vergil nodded to him and kept on beckoning.

"Shit," said Hugh.

He left the window and went into the house by the kitchen door. He went to Vergil, who sat in his chair at the window. He wore his green Boston Celtics jacket over a suit of long underwear. Hugh waited at the door.

"If you pissed yourself again, you're out of luck," Hugh said. "You can wait for her to get back. I ain't doing it."

Vergil nodded to him and waved for him to come closer. The kitchen smelled pleasantly of rising dough.

Hugh went to Vergil's chair.

"Okay," he said. "What is it? What do you want?"

Vergil looked across the kitchen toward the sink. He pointed to the sink. There was nothing in the sink itself except a couple of dirty cups. Hugh thought Vergil was pointing to the coffee can he used for spitting his tobacco, which was on a shelf above the sink. He went to the sink, took the can down, held it out. Vergil shook his head and kept on pointing.

"What? What?" Hugh said.

Then he saw that on the wall above and to one side of the sink was a rack of kitchen knives. Three knives stood point-down in slots in the rack. Hugh touched the knives with his hand. He looked at Vergil. Vergil had sat wearily back in his chair. He nodded.

Hugh took out of the rack a heavy carving knife with a blade a foot long. He weighed it in his hand and turned with it to Vergil. Vergil held out his hand for Hugh to bring him the knife.

Hugh went to Vergil. He held the knife out to Vergil but as Vergil reached for it Hugh pulled it back.

"Wait a minute. What are you doing? What do you want with this?"

Vergil glared at Hugh. He held his hand out for the knife. He was trying to snap his fingers, but he couldn't do it.

"Why?" said Hugh. "What are you going to do?"

Vergil struck his fist down on the arm of his chair and again held out his hand to Hugh. His old jaws worked and under his open jacket his chest rose and fell with the motion of the tireless heart beneath it. But Hugh only looked at him.

"Fuck you," said Hugh. "You want this, you ask her. Ask your girlfriend. Get her to tell me it's okay."

He put the knife in the rack. Then he took all three knives from the rack and started to leave the kitchen. Vergil had fallen back in his chair and shut his eyes. When he opened them, he was looking out the window again.

Hugh stopped before he reached the door. He turned and came back to Vergil. He set the knives on the floor by Vergil's chair and got down on one knee so his face was level with Vergil's. Hugh grasped the arm of Vergil's chair and shook it. Vergil turned to him. Hugh waited, then he said, "You know what I'm doing to him? You know how I've been fucking him?"

Vergil looked at him.

"You'll love it when I tell you," Hugh said. "Get this."

In Condostas' yard under Judgment Hill they were loading one of the big trucks. Marvin stopped the car behind it. A kid neither he nor Mr. Benteen knew saw them and started over.

They were burning the pine slash on the job. Beside the yard and along the muddy track that led up the hill into the remaining woods, big piles of branches and tops smoldered and fumed with a slow, dirty smoke, yellow, gray, black, like smoke from the holes of hell, filling the air with the sharp smell of burning pine.

The kid came up to the car and leaned down to look in the window. He wore a steel hard hat and he stank of sweat, smoke, and gasoline. He put a filthy hand on the door and looked in at them.

"Terry around?" Marvin asked him. Benteen didn't move. He sat looking out the window before him at the stacked logs, the mud, the burning piles.

"Who wants him?"

Marvin smiled at him.

"Nobody, I guess," he said. "We were going by. You're burning off."

"Looks that way," said the kid.

"You must be about done," Marvin said.

The kid was looking at Benteen, who sat like a stone man.

"Terry's up there," he said. "They poured the cellar but they never drained it. Forgot. Do you believe it? Now the sucker's full of water. Terry's going to shit if he has to pump it. Must be two feet of water in it, going nowhere. Terry's hot."

Marvin nodded.

"He'll be down sometime, you want to wait," the kid said.

"We were driving by," Marvin said.

"What's the matter with him?" the kid asked.

"Nothing," said Marvin.

The kid was looking in at the leather interior of the car. He slid his hand over the hood outside.

"Your rig?" he asked Marvin.

"His," said Marvin.

"Nice."

He turned his head and spat into the mud beside the car. He pushed himself back from the window and walked away.

"He's a winner, ain't he?" Marvin said. "I wonder who he is. Might be one of Junior Benware's."

"He's no Benware," Benteen said. "He's nobody. He's new. Look at this. He's made a junkyard out of this."

It was true. Not only was the yard a mire and the air foul, but the ground, between the ruined trees and raw stumps, was bright with cast-off oil cans, foam coffee cups, hamburger boxes, soft drink cans, beer cans, plastic bottles, glass bottles, candy wrappers, cigarette packages, and ribbons of toilet paper. Some of the stuff had been dropped by the men, some had blown in from the road. Off to the side of the yard there was even an old refrigerator that somebody had used this clearing to dispose of.

"Maybe he'll clean it up, when they get done," Marvin said.

"Why should he?" Benteen asked.

At the top of the track Terry Condosta appeared, on foot. Marvin and Benteen knew him by the white cowboy hat he wore. Terry stood up there and looked down the hill at them.

"You want me to go get him?" Marvin asked.

"Across the brook," Benteen said, "there's a place you can stand, look right down on top of this. He's putting in a house. You can't see it from here. I was up there. Down here, he's going around in his god damned hat, bossing everybody around, had no idea I was watching him."

Marvin lifted his arm and waved to Terry, but Terry didn't wave back. He stood in the log track at the top of the hill and looked down at them.

"What do you reckon he is, there?" Benteen asked. "Hundred yards?"

"Less," said Marvin. "Fifty, seventy-five."

"That close?"

Terry had started walking down the track toward them.

"You seen his truck?" Benteen asked. "He's got the door lettered: Leisureland. T C Leisureland."

"T. C.," Marvin said. "Terry Condosta."

"Get me out of here," Benteen said.

"You don't want to talk to him?" Marvin asked.

"I tried to buy this," Benteen said. "I talked to Marco. I offered to take the whole piece. He didn't even figure to make out here, he said. But he wouldn't do it."

"You told me," Marvin said.

"Here is what happens," Benteen said. "Here it is. Right here. You see it. This is no drill. Could I have stopped it?"

"No," Marvin said. "If you got to buy it it don't count."

"What?" Benteen said. "What did you say?"

Terry Condosta walking down the steep track among the wreckage of the woods. In the yard below, Marvin starting the car, backing around, and heading for the road. Terry stopping, watching them drive off, turning back up the hill.

* * *

"What? What did you say?"

That was Thursday. Then Monday he called again. The same fellow. I knew who it was right away, although this time he sounded a little different. Not so pert.

Ah, ah, may I speak to Hugh, please?

No, you can't, I said. He's working. What do you want?

Ah. My name's Guest. I called the other day.

I know who you are, I said. I've been hearing from you a good deal more than I need to, I said. What do you want with him?

Look here, Mrs. Blankenship, it's important I speak to Hugh. Is there a number you can give me where I can reach him?

No, there ain't, I said. He's haying. Now you listen to me—

Tell Hugh to stand down, he said. Tell him to drop the project. Simply drop it. Our friend is too close. Our friend will be waiting for him if he moves. He will be waiting for

172

Hugh. So Hugh must stand down. Is that clear? Do you have that? Tell him that.

Now you listen to me, I said. I'm not going to tell anybody anything until you tell me some things. Who are you? What do you have to do with my son? If I don't get some answers from you fast, I'm calling the police. Have you got that?

And he said in that fancy voice of his: At this particular point, Mrs. Blankenship, calling the police would be quite superfluous, I'm sorry to say. Some such smart remark as that.

What does that mean? I said. Now you listen to me . . .

But he had hung up. And in a way, that's the reason everything worked out the way it did for us. I knew he was trouble, and I was right about that. I didn't want him and Hugh to have anything to do with each other, and I was right about that, too. And so that's why I didn't say anything about that second call, and I wasn't right about that. I wish I had. If I had, things would have been different. Or maybe not.

Althea was in the yard. She waved when they drove up, then went to the house ahead of them and waited at the door. She shook hands with Mr. Benteen the way she did every time. She looked at Tyler once, then at Benteen again.

"She's my new driver," Benteen said.

"Sure, she is," Althea said. "Course."

"What's going on?" Benteen asked her.

"That boy?" said Althea. "That boy was here yesterday,

173

for the wood. I went over to my sister's for an hour. She's got her back bothering, she could hardly move and I said I'd help her with her wash while he was over here."

"All right," said Benteen.

"When I got back," Althea said, "it seemed like he'd wanted the boy to get him a knife down from the wall. He wanted one of those butcher knives we have. The boy got it down, all right, then he thought better of it and didn't give it to him. That's all."

"How's Aurora?" Benteen asked.

"Some better today," Althea said. "It's where she had her disc operation, it didn't make her better. Made her worse. Now they want to do another operation. I don't know."

"Well," Benteen said. "Let's have a look at him."

He went into the kitchen, leaving the two women at the door. Tyler waited for Althea to go in before her, but Althea stood back.

"Go ahead in," said Althea. "You go on ahead. He won't hurt you. Goodness sake."

Vergil was at his window. He looked up when Benteen came into the room but when he saw Tyler behind him he forgot about Benteen. He watched her. She waited inside the door and let Althea go around her and stand behind Vergil and Benteen.

"I took them right out of here," Althea said. "That boy handed them to me and I took them right out to the shed. That's where they're staying."

Vergil was looking around at Tyler. He was trying to get turned in his chair so he could see her better.

"Come on over here where he can see you," Benteen said. Tyler went to them and sat in a kitchen chair that Althea placed for her near the window. Vergil watched her.

"Yes," said Althea to Vergil. "There she is. Ain't she a pretty thing?"

"He don't talk," Benteen said.

"I know," said Tyler. "Mrs. Blankenship said."

"Oh," said Althea. "She's the new girl living at Cordie's."

"Was living there," said Benteen.

"That's right," said Althea. She nodded. She smiled at them through her heavy glasses. "That's right. Now I mind."

"She lives with me now," Benteen said. He was talking to Vergil, not Althea. "She's my driver," he said. "She drives my car. You know my car? I had that kid was out here for a driver. I fired him. He wasn't paying attention so I fired him. I busted him right down to hay hand. Now I got her. What do you think about that?"

Vergil looked from Tyler to Benteen. Althea stood behind Vergil's chair and grinned through her glasses down at the three of them.

"What do you think?" Benteen said to Vergil. "Did I do right? She look like a driver to you? Does she?"

"All right," said Tyler. "All right. What is this?"

"No," Benteen said. "No, she don't to me, either. She's no driver. She's something else. What? What is she, do you reckon?"

Vergil turned to look at Tyler again.

"What are you doing?" Tyler asked Benteen. "God, what are you doing now?"

"She's no driver," said Benteen. "She's no whore. She's no thief. She's got a man in jail in Texas but she's no outlaw. I'm god damned if I know what she is. You tell me what she is."

"I'm getting out of here," Tyler said. But she kept her seat.

"Don't mind," Althea said. "It don't matter. He don't understand much of it."

"He understands plenty," said Benteen. "Don't you? Don't you? This is no drill and he knows it. He understands plenty, but he don't say. Do you? What do you think? I fired that kid and took her on and now I don't know what I got and you won't tell me."

Vergil looked at him. He blinked. He yawned and looked away out the window. He was sleepy. He seemed to have forgotten Tyler. Vergil's attention, or his pale old gaze, had the quality that it fixed objects effortfully, one at a time, and lost them utterly when it moved on.

"Ah," said Benteen. "It don't matter. It ain't real. Come on, let's see the god damned birds."

"That's it," Althea said. "We got some new ones today."

Benteen turned to Vergil again.

"Said you went for a knife," he said. "What were you playing at, there? Butcher knife, she said. What did you want with a butcher knife? Were you going to cut some meat?"

Vergil put out his hand to the windowsill for the bird book that lay there. He couldn't quite reach it.

"He wants his book," Althea said, and Tyler, who sat closest, picked it up and handed it to Vergil. He took it from her, but he didn't look at her. His mind was on the book now. He opened it on his lap and went through it 'til he found the plate he wanted.

"That's a new one," Benteen said. "Owls. Those are old owls you got, there."

"Big ones," said Althea.

"Great gray owl." Benteen read. "Great horned owl. Hell, I've seen them, right around here. What happened to those others, those parrots, those shiny ones of yours?"

"Seems like all the brighty ones are gone," said Althea. "All it is is owls, owls, owls the last two, three days."

"Must be the other ones went south," said Benteen.

"That's right," Althea said. She grinned and shook her head. "My, aren't we having a good time?"

"You reckon those others went south?" Benteen said to Vergil.

Vergil pointed to the page of owls, their bent shoulders, their great, dangerous eyes, their wide wings nearly the size of a man's stretched-out arms. The great gray owl's wings span five feet: a bird the size of a boy.

"That's that gray owl," Althea said. "He's the biggest."

"You want to watch him," said Benteen. "He'll come around, pick you right up like a rabbit."

Vergil looked at him, looked at Tyler, at Althea.

"Thing that size?" Benteen said. "Pick you right up like you were a baby. Carry you away."

"Stop it," said Tyler.

Benteen looked at her.

"What's the matter with you?" he said.

"You're scaring him, can't you see?" said Tyler. "You're scaring him to death."

I told him. I fucking told him, sure I did. Vergil. Laid the whole thing out for him. It's perfect, because who's Vergil going to tell? He can't talk. It's like telling a dog or a cat. Or no: it's like writing it all down and then hiding it where nobody can ever find it.

Because I've been wanting to tell it. I pretty nearly told it to Debbie Does Dallas back there, but something made me shut up. Good thing. Last thing I need is her blabbing to Garrett now she's out there with him. I don't think there's much danger of that kind of thing with Vergil, do you? Not unless that Althea gets him going so he kind of finds his voice, sings out, at the last second when she makes him pop his cracker—only then, like the dying swan. I could be in trouble then, but I'm not worried.

The thing is, the man is a pro, and Terry never liked it, always worried, worried. Wished he'd never gotten into it in the first place. Then when his truck—his dad's truck—dumps he bails out. Chickenshit. Not the man, no, the man has nerves of ice. No nerves at all. But he's a pro, he's a businessman. Clever, he's a clever old boy and his idea is: they never know. You can't go down for stealing something nobody knows is gone.

But in a way, in a way, you know, then—what's the point?

Sure, you've got to get away. Sure, you've got to get the money. That's why you're doing it, right? So the man fixes it up with great care, so it's a secret: the fake weather vane, the ropes, so on. Sure, that's smart. It's got to be a secret. But forever? So nobody knows, ever? In a way, why do it at all, then? In a way, if nobody ever finds out about it, what's it mean?

So I gave it to Vergil, the whole thing. Thinking about telling Boomer, too. Not now, but when it's done and I'm out of here, long gone. Send him a postcard. *Dear Boomer* . . . . That pussy.

Who I'd really like to tell is Marv. I can hear him. I'd tell him. He'd say, *You did what? How did you do that?* I'd tell him the whole thing, the fake ram, this rope, that rope, going up there, coming down, going up again. I know what Marv would say like I heard it. He'd say:

Well, what did you want to do all that for?

Daddy, Daddy, Daddy, she had said. Let me tell you about my daddy sometime. Then she said, No.

No. Not up here among the serried hills, steeple-pierced,

the abandoned farms, the unabandoned farms, the villages that were what they had been and what the thing they had been had become, the swift little brooks everywhere, the bird-thronged woods, the narrow valleys that held back the sky. No sky, no chili, no oil, no JESUS IS LORD. No friends. That was no country for her Daddy. And even if it had been, it was too late. For in fact her Daddy had moved on. He wasn't there at all. Wild Bill was gone.

Friends, Wild Bill said. You get along by having friends. Your daughter is your friend; you're hers. It's all about friends. But when you have had the last friend and he has had you; when you have taken care of all your friends and they have taken care of you; when the homes have gotten poorer and poorer, the commerce meaner and meaner, when the salt has lost its savor, then what? What's next? Nobody knows. There are no rules.

Make sure you know what's true. Get it all right. Then change one thing: that's what Wild Bill said. Know it all, then change one thing. Change one thing—if you can. What if you can't? You've got no rules.

Therefore, if Wild Bill, no longer living beside a golf course with a fake Scotch name—no longer, even, living in a county next to a county that had a golf course by any name at all—if Wild Bill one morning took a revolver out to the garage, well, he wasn't the first and he won't be the last.

The sheriff had been Wild Bill's friend. He drove over himself to tell Penelope. She saw his cruiser stop at the curb in front of the bank where she was working in Corsicana.

* * *

Tyler got behind the wheel of Mr. Benteen's Mercedes. She turned on the engine. Then she turned it off.

"Are you going to tell me what that was all about in there?" she asked Benteen.

"You know what it was about," said Benteen. "Start the car."

"You talked like I was trying to do you in," Tyler said.

"You know what you're trying to do," said Benteen. "Go ahead. Get me out of here."

Tyler started the car and they drove out of Vergil's yard, into the lane, and out to the road. There Tyler waited.

"Which way?" she asked. "Home?"

"You know which way." Benteen said. "You know what happens now."

Tyler went right on the road and started back by the way that led past Condostas' cutting on Judgment Hill and so to Benteens'.

"I don't want to hear that," Tyler said. "I don't want to hear that from you. You sound like him, with that. You know? You sound just like Hulon. 'You know what I mean,' and 'You know what happens.' That's like what Hulon says."

"Maybe he's right," Benteen said. "Are you afraid, now? Are you afraid of me, now?"

"No," said Tyler. "I'm not afraid of him and I'm not afraid of you."

On the right, now, in a haze of smoke from the burning slash, the wasteland at the bottom of Condostas' job; on the left, the Dead River branch and across it the woods where Benteen's land ended at the water of the brook.

"Turn off here," said Benteen. "Stop the car. Let me out."

"What?" Tyler said. "Why? No. What are you doing?"

"Do what I tell you," Benteen said. "Get over there. Go ahead, do it. Do it now."

Mr. Benteen crossed the branch on dry stones. He went up the bank away from the road until the woods hid him, then stopped and turned to look behind him. He saw Tyler drive away. He started back toward the brook and the road, but when he heard a car coming he dropped down out of sight and let it pass. He was hiding. On his own land, he was hiding. He didn't know why.

He got back over the brook, crossed the road again, and stood in the log landing where Condosta's trucks loaded. Nobody was there, no vehicles. He stood and listened but he could hear no sound: no saws, no machinery, no voices. Beside the yard and along the tracks that led up into what was left of the woods the slash piles still burned, but weakly, smoldering now without fire or heat, with nothing but a thin blue smoke. They would burn that way for days.

Benteen began walking up the track farthest to the right, which would take him to the new cellar they had put in. The skidders' enormous tires and the logs they dragged had gouged the track deep into the hillside, and Benteen walked in a gully between high dirt walls hung with ragged, torn-out tree roots, scarred, busted ledge, and raw boulders. The scattered trash of papers, bottles, cans lay all about him and he kicked it as he walked. He looked around him, dumb, a starved, exhausted survivor returned to the ruins of his city, his broken street. Above the skidder track the woods that remained were scrawny and let in a watery light. The big trees were gone and half the little ones were smashed. That odd yellow light lay curiously among the injured trees and among hundreds, thousands of big stumps oozing sap and gum, over which the flies and hornets buzzed.

Where the track leveled out, Benteen slowed his walk and went softly. He didn't know but what somebody would be working at the house site, though he had heard nothing from below. He stopped and listened again. He went on until he had the cellar in sight through the poor trees that had been left by the loggers. Nobody there.

Fifty feet from the new cellar the track he followed came to an old stone wall that lay across its path to the house site. The skidder, bulldozer, or whatever it was that had made the track had simply gone through the wall, knocked it down, scattered its stones, and shoved them out of the way to either side. Benteen stopped at the fallen wall. He picked up one or two of the smaller stones and set them back in the broken ends of the wall, but mostly the stones were too big for him. The biggest he could see was a long granite slab the size of a camp bed. A stone that big might weigh a thousand pounds. Two or three men and a horse would have worked to throw that old son-of-a-bitch up into the wall. Condosta's operator had moved it out of his way as if it had been a cobweb.

Here they come. This is no drill.

They had poured the cellar and taken away the forms. The gray concrete curb stuck up above the dirt and mud. Beside the cellar one of Condostas' skidders hunched like a stegosaur. Another one was parked back in the woods to one side. Benteen went to the skidder and laid his hand on the blade mounted at the front. It was cold as a stone though the day was coming in hot. The cellar, he saw, had a foot of water at the bottom of it, and the water was full of fat tadpoles rushing here and there in gangs, like blackbirds.

Whose place had this been? He knew who had wrecked it. Well, he didn't know, but he knew it didn't matter: some kid sitting up on a big machine had wrecked the place, some nameless kid, a stranger, no blood even of the degraded Benwares. Someone lower than Benwares had destroyed it. But who had made it?

"Something you want?"

It wasn't the wild that Mr. Benteen would hold, would fix, would save if he could. It wasn't wilderness. What of wilderness he'd seen, the long, poor spruce townships of Maine, of Quebec, he could not care for. He had an obscurer object of care, a more difficult one, not land merely but a setting, a human world, palimpsest: the woods that had been farm that had been woods, the laboriously piled walls, the empty cellar holes, fallen chimneys, rock piles, the pounds, the stoneyards—the oaks and beeches and grapevines that covered them over like a temple in the jungle, owls and foxes living in what had been halls of men.

Whose place had this been? It wasn't their life he wanted to hold, to know, and it wasn't the past, not quite, but an image that partook vainly of both: men, women, and children, working, busy right here, now gone. He cared for them and for their fading sign, a country where men had labored and then for whatever reason had quit their labor and gone away, a country in transition.

"I said, something you want here? Huh? What do you want here?"

Terry Condosta stood ten feet behind Benteen. He'd come up the track from the landing on foot. With him was Lower-than-Benwares, the kid who had admired Benteen's car a couple of days earlier. Terry stuck his hands in the back pockets of his jeans and leaned toward Benteen like a bad dog on a chain. The wide brim of his cowboy hat snapped at the air between them, but Terry let that interval of air stay ten feet long. He didn't come any closer.

"So?" Terry said again.

"What?" asked Benteen.

"Are you looking for me?" Terry asked. "You were here the other day, weren't you? I saw you. I saw you and Bland then, I saw you in that Benz. What do you want? Do you want to see me?"

"You?" Benteen said. "No."

"Then you're trespassing, aren't you?" said Terry. "You're trespassing here."

"No," said Benteen. He turned from them and started to leave.

"Wait a minute," Terry said. "Did you hear me? Are you drunk? Are you drunk, again? You're going to tell me what you want with me, what you're doing trespassing here. Wait."

But Benteen had left the cellar and started down the hill toward the road, not by the track he had come up but straight down the hill, among the stumps and busted saplings.

"Where do you think you're going?" Terry called after him. "Go get him," he said to the kid with him. "Go after him. Stop him."

"Hey, fuck you," the kid said. "Stop him yourself. I ain't going anywhere near him."

He and Terry watched Benteen stumble down the hill through the ruined woods. He went on down to the road, crossed a little way from where he'd crossed earlier, out of sight of them now. Benteen got over the branch and back in the woods on his own place—woods where there was no trespass, woods where the skidders wouldn't come.

Woods where they wouldn't have to.

If you got to buy it it don't count.

The cupola on top of the barn at Benteens' didn't have a floor. There were open joists, a kind of catwalk you could stand on and look down between your shoes forty feet to the deck of the hayloft, swallows dipping in and out by the loft door below you. You climbed up there on cleats nailed to the big posts, then on a narrow ladder.

Hugh tied one end of his rope to a stud inside the cupola and left the rest in a big coil on the catwalk. He could pass the free end between the louvers of the window opposite and let it down. Now he looked carefully out. The yard, far below, was empty. Marvin was in the tractor shed. He was running the torch. Hugh could hear it. Benteen and Debbie Does Dallas had gone off in the Benz.

Hugh had got the rope and made his move. Ten o'clock, getting ready for a hot one. Hugh could see the bottom of the pasture, where the cows were already looking for shade. Light, white clouds, unmoving. The hills in a blue haze, the farthest ones invisible.

Hugh went down the little ladder to a crossbeam, then down the post to the hayloft. There he waited again, listened. Then he started to climb down the loft ladder to the ground. When he was most of the way down, Tyler came into the barn in a hurry.

"Where's Marvin?" she asked.

"He's around," Hugh said. "What's the matter with you?" He was waiting for her to ask him what he'd been doing up the tower there.

"He took off," she said. "He made me pull over down the road, then he took off into the woods."

"Garrett?"

"He's run off," Tyler said.

"Is that right?" said Hugh. "Well, I wouldn't worry about him too much, you know? He knows the woods. He'll be back."

"No," Tyler said. "No, you didn't see him. Where's Marvin?"

"I don't have to see him," said Hugh. "I told you he'd hit the wall. Don't worry about him. He'll turn up, and if he don't, we'll go get him. It's happened before. You know, what Garrett needs is a good fuck. You too, maybe, by now. What do you think?"

"Where's Marvin?"

"I've seen you out there on the porch, you know," Hugh said. "Night after night with him. He ain't that interesting. Talk, talk, talk. Jesus, I liked to died of boredom."

"You talk some yourself," Tyler said.

"But that ain't all I do," said Hugh. "Is it? I got other bullets in my gun. Unlike Garrett. You know I have. You know once you had a farmboy you can never go back."

Marvin came into the barn by the big doors.

"Ain't that right, Marv?" said Hugh. "She tries one of us, she'll never go back?"

Marvin stopped. He looked at Tyler.

"I thought that was you," he said. "Where's Garrett?"

He didn't have the legs any more. The rest he had as good as ever, well, as good as he needed it, but not the legs. He would get on top of the hill where it was an easy half-hour home. There he would stop and blow for ten minutes. Noon. Marvin would be wondering about him. She'd get home, Marvin would ask her, Where's Garrett? I don't know, she'd say, he went to the woods. When? Marvin would ask. Or he'd ask the kid, Where's Garrett? The kid having no idea at all, on the moon, thinking himself alone in the world the way any kid does—thinking wrong.

Gone to the woods, the intact woods, the inviolate woods, the saving remnant, his woods, his land. Gone to the woods? When? Which way?

The wooded hill went up like stairs: a rise, a flat, another rise. The woods were empty at midday, no singing birds, no rustling animal steps. Benteen climbed through them like the last creature on earth. All about him stone walls ran off into the woods, some across the slope, some going right up and down. The walls looked so straight, met and crossed in such good order, that you wanted to follow them like streets, but if you did you would soon become lost. Benteen's woods were full of the bones of deer hunters, fugitives, lovers, Boy Scouts, Girl Scouts who had thought they could follow a wall out of the woods and had wandered and perished, because the walls, straight as they looked, weren't streets: they didn't go anywhere except to other walls. You had to ignore the walls and keep right up the pitch of the hill to the top. There you found top-of-the-woods, then the track down to the road, then you were all right. If you got lost in that country you followed water, not the walls.

Benteen reached the top of the hill, a breezy open woods on broken ground grown over between the trees with long tough grass like hair. He found the path. Ahead the woods closed in again some, but he could see beyond that where broad yellow light lay in the open: top-of-the-woods. He went through the trees and stopped at the edge of the mowing. He sat under a tree, stretched his legs out in front of him, shut his eyes. Somewhere off down the hill crows were carrying on, black crows cawing in the treetops, their wings flapping, and on his left, nearby, the sound of running water in a brook or spring, some kind of water.

Every city is built over rivers, streams. The city builds itself over them, over everything, spreading like ink. How many rivers run under the streets of New York, of London, of Rome? They are forgotten except by the engineers. For the city that would one day rise right here, they would cut the trees and dig up the grass as they had across the branch, but then they wouldn't stop and leave a wasteland behind. They would go on. They would lay out streets and build the buildings of a city right here. On top of the hills and in the valleys between the hills they would build it. If a hillside should be too steep they would grade it down and build. They would bury the rivers, make them run in pipes and in stone channels under the streets. The rivers would still be there, because you can't make a river go away, but they would be buried, changed, and nobody would know what they were.

Something like the same thing would become of the other permanent life of the countryside, the animals and birds of the woods, fields, and farms. They wouldn't disappear, but they would become people, the different people of the city: workers, cops, taxi drivers, businessmen, messengers, window washers, panhandlers, the animal life of the country become men and women with different names, different jobs, as in a book for little boys and girls. It would happen. It would happen right here. A country in transition is in transition toward the city, never away from it.

That's how Hugh found Mr. Benteen asleep under a tree at the edge of the top piece. His back against a tree, his legs spread out before him, his mouth open. He might have been any old bum. All he lacked was the wine bottle.

"Shit," said Hugh. He looked down at Benteen. Then he got down on one knee, took him by the ankle, and shook him a little.

"Shit, what are you doing?" Hugh said. "Let's go. Come on. What are you doing up here? Let's go, okay? I don't have time for this. This is my big night, you know? Tonight's show time. Hey, let's go. Let's go, now."

Benteen looked at him. He blinked. He looked at him.

"Get me out of here," he said.

If you got to buy it it don't count.

Get me out of here. Get me out of here, he's saying. Fuck it. Just fuck it all. Because that was it. That's what it was.

My big night coming up and he has to pick that same day to crash and burn. Five o'clock in the afternoon and I'm way to hell up on top-of-the-woods with him and him like a bag full of marbles. He's been up there for anyway seven, eight hours. Course he couldn't walk, was making no sense, was all stove in from running around out there and then conking out in the woods. If I hadn't brought the truck, he'd been up there yet.

He couldn't walk. I had to help him. I don't know what these old fuckers up here are going to do when I'm gone and can't carry them around. Crawl, I guess. I didn't really carry him, no, although I could, he ain't that big, but I got him on his feet and kind of got under his arm and walked him to the truck.

Where the hell have you been? I said. We been looking for you all afternoon. Nobody got nothing done all day.

So what? he said, Nobody gets nothing done anyway.

Gratitude, boy. It's a beautiful thing.

Hey, I said, you like it up here so much, maybe I'll put you back down, huh? You can go back to sleep? Maybe die of exposure?

Get me out of here, he said, and that's the last out of him I heard. By the time I got him in the truck and we got back down to the place he was past talking.

So we went back on down, near dinnertime now, and yes, there pulled in behind the tractor barn, out of sight, is Rackstraw's cruiser. And, yes, I did think, What? but I thought he'd come out to help look for Garrett and so I went ahead. Him missing since morning, me finding him, me the one bringing him home. Any other time I'd have wondered why

Rackstraw would want to hide his cruiser if all he was doing was just helping look, but that night with Garrett I didn't. I didn't think about it. And that's what it was.

They got Mr. Benteen into the house, got him on his bed, got his shoes off. He didn't seem as though he hurt, but his legs were gone. His legs were gone and he wouldn't talk to them. He lay on his bed looking around him, looking at Marvin and Tyler, not saying a word. After a while he went to sleep. They put a cover over him. They went out onto the porch where Hugh was waiting.

"I'm going to call the doctor," Tyler said.

"He don't need a doctor," Marvin said. "Let him be alone. Let him sleep. Maybe get him something to eat later. Keep an eye on him. He's okay."

"If he's okay, I'm going," Hugh said.

"Go ahead," said Marvin.

"I'm going to the movie," Hugh said.

"Is that right?"

"It starts at seven, I got to get cleaned up, get down there by seven. Then, after, I'm going on down, they're having a band."

"Go on, then," said Marvin.

"I won't be back 'til real late, probably," Hugh said.

Marvin looked at him. "Okay," said Marvin. "Go ahead if you're going. Nobody's in your way."

Hugh left. Marvin went back into the house to look in on Benteen. He had turned onto his side and was fast asleep. Marvin went back to the porch.

"Take a look at him from time to time," Marvin said. "When he wakes up, he'll be hungry. When he's eaten he'll go back to sleep. Then tomorrow, tomorrow night, that's when we keep an eye on him."

"For what?" Tyler asked.

"For whatever's next," Marvin said. "He ain't done yet."

"How do you know?" Tyler asked.

"I can tell," Marvin said.

Marvin stayed with her at Benteens' until it got dark. Benteen didn't wake. Marvin went home about nine. Tyler sat on the porch by herself. She sat out there for an hour. Then she went to his room and sat in a chair in a corner. Benteen was asleep on his side with his back to her. She got up from her chair and went to the bed. She leaned over Benteen so she could see his face. He slept.

"Where are you?" Tyler whispered. "What's on your mind? How much do you know?"

Of course he couldn't hear her. He breathed easily in sleep.

"You're a funny man," Tyler whispered. "You get what you want. You get what you don't want."

She touched Benteen's shoulder. He didn't stir.

"You're a funny man, but I've got you," Tyler said. "I know you. Oh, yes, I do. I know you and I've got you now."

Past midnight she decided to get what sleep she could in there, rather than go to her own room and leave him alone, so she brought a soft chair from the book room. She slept fitfully, expecting Benteen to wake, having no idea what she'd do if he woke, but he didn't wake. Benteen slept on even when shouting from outside, from the barn, woke Tyler—shouting, breaking glass, then a gunshot, then more shouting, running steps, then another gunshot. Tyler sat up in her chair with her heart trying to leap out of her chest, but Benteen never moved.

Deputy Rackstraw jumped the gun. He was never a patient man. He waited as long as he could. He waited, first, for hours while nothing at all happened, sitting in the shadows of the tractor shed where he could see the yard and the barn. He waited while Hugh at last arrived, long past midnight, walked across the dark yard and went into the barn, climbed to the cupola, let down his rope. He waited while Hugh reappeared at the barn door with Mr. Guest's tin ram slung across his back and a coil of rope over his shoulder, went around the side, climbed his rope to the roof, to the cupola, unbolted Benteen's golden ram from up there, put the new one in its place, lowered Benteen's ram on the second rope, and got ready to climb back down himself. The deputy waited until Hugh had come down off the pitch of the roof and was hanging under the eaves against the wall, thirty feet in the air. Then he left the shed and went quickly to the barn. He stood at the bottom of the rope Hugh was climbing down. He spoke to the shadow of the wall at the top of the rope.

"All right," the deputy said. "That's good. Right there."

He ought to have let Hugh get all the way down the rope. At the top of the wall on that side of the big barn at Benteens', under the eaves, was a row of clerestory windows intended to let light and air into the loft. Hugh was about level with them the deputy called him out. Hugh looked down and saw the deputy waiting for him. He pushed off the wall with his legs and swung back in on the rope, hitting one of the windows and going right through it, feet first. He dropped the rope and landed on the deck of the loft, inside the barn, in a storm of glass and splintered wood and flakes of old paint and dust.

The deputy ran around the corner of the barn to the

front. He went in the big doors and stopped. He heard Hugh's running steps pounding on the deck of the loft overhead. He drew his sidearm and entered the barn.

"Right there!" the deputy shouted. But Hugh, above, kept on running.

The deputy raised his revolver and fired a shot into the air. Inside the big barn, the shot sounded like the end of the world. For a moment the deputy was deafened. Hugh's steps overhead had stopped; anyway he couldn't hear them. He had fired at random, but his shot had to have gone clear through the deck of the loft. He might have hit him. The deputy knew there were stairs to the loft in the corner. He went toward it, tripping over things in the dark.

He found the steps and went up, but the second his head and shoulders came above the level of the loft floor, Hugh broke out of the shadows at the corner of the loft and ran flat out for the loading doors at the front.

"Right there!" the deputy shouted. "Right there!"

He came the rest of the way up the ladder and ran after Hugh in the dark, their booted feet like thunder on the boards of the empty loft. Hugh reached the loading doors and kept right on going, out into the air. It was a twenty-foot fall, but Marvin's wagon stacked with baled hay was pulled in below. Hugh landed on the bales easily, rolled, and dropped to the yard as the deputy and his revolver reached the loading door above.

The deputy stopped in the loading door. He didn't jump. Outside, in the yard below him, Hugh was running hard toward the tractor shed. If he got around there he was among the coops and piggeries, then trees, then the road. The deputy had one move left. He didn't want to take it. Yes, he did. He raised his revolver in both hands, braced it against the side of the loading door, put the barrel on Hugh's running figure down in the yard, let out his breath, and fired. But Hugh was around the corner and gone. That was no warning shot the deputy fired at him from the high door, but Hugh was gone around the shed, and all the deputy saw, by the starlight that fell on the yard at Benteens' that famous night, was the windshield of his own vehicle, his cruiser, parked at the corner of the shed, turn in an instant white as milk.

PART IV

"I'm right outside, here," Althea said. "I'm out here on the porch cleaning peas. You want a pea before I start? . . . I guess not. I'm right out here. You tap on the window, I'll hear you."

Vergil paid her no mind. Across the yard into the woods a lot of them were getting up to something.

"You just sit tight in here," Althea said. "You need anything, tap right on the glass, I'll come. I don't want to see nothing like when that boy was out here. You about scared me to death."

Vergil was trying to see them. He couldn't quite make them out. They were inside the trees across his yard, and the old wavy window glass he had to look through bent the trees and shadows when Vergil tried to see. Wait. There they were. And, as he'd thought, they were the old-time ones now, no longer were they the fancy, made-up birds of the south; these were the real thing, the old-time birds he knew: jays, they were, and some other birds, crying and squawking and clamoring around something in the treetops. Crows, too, black as coal. They flew in and out of the woods, rising into the sky, then descending again to the upper branches, crawking and carrying on the whole time. Vergil could see a kind of dark shape in the branches there, but he wasn't sure that was what they were after.

Where had those shiny ones got to? Well, they didn't belong around here at all, never had. It must be they'd gone away. They'd never had any business way up here, he knew. They were make-believe, maybe. Not these.

Very likely it was an owl they had surprised. Those jays, those crows, if they came on one of the big brown owls by day when it was blind and stupid, would gather around it and abuse it and chase it and generally give it hell, mad because at night the owl would be after them. They would gang up on it. Birds are like that, they stick together, live together, even move together like one thing, one bird. You saw them like that, all kinds: four of them sitting on a wire, they all fly away in the same half a second; a hundred flying in a flock, they all turn at the same second and flash their bellies like metal in the sun, like silver, all at once. Vergil had seen whole fields, right here, full of seagulls. Yes, seagulls. You turned over a field and seagulls, by Christ, would come, hundreds of them, right here in town. From where? It must be two hundred miles from any sea, a long way, anyhow. He'd seen whole fields full of white seagulls moving over the black, steaming earth.

Now the birds in the woods, or whatever they were chasing, had moved closer to the edge of the trees. They were screaming and dashing around in there, there might have been a dozen of them, and he bent toward the window to see what it was that had them going.

Wait. There it was, a big one, too. It came stumbling out of the trees, flapping, heavy, blind, and flew right for his window, a dozen lesser birds, a thousand lesser birds, a million after it, shrieking at it, driving it. Here they come. See? See it now?

* * *

Ten, fifteen minutes later Althea finished shelling out her peas and came back into the kitchen. She went to the sink and put the pan of peas down and turned on the water.

"It's cool out there, you know it?" said Althea. "You get out of the sun, it's cool."

She looked over at Vergil. She turned the water off and took up a towel. She looked at him again, put her head on one side and looked some more. She didn't go to him right away. She dried her hands in the towel. She went to his chair. She bent over him and looked into his face.

"Well, well, look at you," said Althea. "Look at you, now."

She crossed the kitchen to the corner where she had had them put the telephone.

W‌ell, my heart went down like an elevator. *Whump*. Like that. The first thing I find that morning, Tuesday morning, is he's not in his room, not in the house at all. His bed not slept in. He said he was going to the movie.

Okay.

Then right away here's somebody banging on the door and I go down and there's Buddy Rackstraw in, what do you call it, full fig, with the uniform, the belt, the boots, the funny hat, and so help me he's got his hand on his gun.

Well, it being Buddy, of course the first thing I thought was, Oh, Lord, he's crashed his car and they've come to tell me. He's out on the highway someplace. But no.

Where's Hugh? says Buddy.

Not here, I said. What's the matter?

So Buddy goes into this business about him catching Hugh stealing the weather vane off Benteens' barn last night and chasing him and losing him and now he's got the state police out and some big antique thief in Boston. No, a whole ring of thieves and Hugh did this and Terry Condosta did that, and Hugh, and so on.

Now, wait a minute, I said. Hold it. I don't know anything about anything you're talking about and he don't either. I never heard anything so ridiculous in my life, I said, but when he said about that big thief and Boston, my heart landed at the bottom of my stomach. I didn't want to talk at all, to anybody. Still, though, he's okay, he's not dead on the highway, so that's something gained. And then I guess I found my tongue. I kind of took up, and I put it right back to Buddy. It worked, too, and I saw it was working and I kind of warmed to it. I have seldom lacked long for words.

Let me see if I've got this right, I said. You got him climbing around on a rope on the roof of Benteens' barn with a weather vane, and then there's another weather vane, right? A second weather vane? Course, there is. And then there's some big conspiracy, is that right? A gang that steals weather vanes, is that it? You figure those are the same guys that shot Kennedy, or what?

I saw him, Buddy said. Where is he?

I don't know what you saw, I said, and I don't think you do, either. Some people think because they got a job with the sheriff's office they can throw their weight around and intimidate people. Well, that don't work around here. You can get on your way now.

If you know where he is and you don't say, you're an accessory, Buddy said. You can get in trouble, too. It don't matter that you're his mom. The judge don't care.

My, my, I said. Is that right? Well I guess I'll just have to take my chances, won't I? Now you get out of here.

I just want to talk to him, said Buddy.

Buddy never was up to much. My Daddy taught him in school, he taught them all. About Buddy Rackstraw, Daddy said he had the brains of a '49 Ford.

If I see him I'll tell him you'd like to talk to him, I said. Now for the last time, you get off my property.

Or what? Buddy said. You going to call the deputy? Real cagey.

You don't want to find out what I'm going to do, I said. And he kind of hitched his belt and went back to his car.

Not up to much, no. When Daddy heard Buddy Rackstraw had been taken on as a deputy, he shook his head. Does that mean they'll give him a firearm? he asked. And they told him that's what it looked like, and Daddy shook his head and said God save the mark.

Benteen woke at dawn. He had slept for a night and a day and a night. Now he knew he was in his own bed but that was all he knew. He sat up and began to dress himself.

Outside in the lane that led down from the barn, he found Vergil on his way to top-of-the-woods with his brother's .22 to shoot a rabbit.

You can't hit a rabbit with that thing, said Benteen. Nobody can. Vergil didn't answer him but turned into the bottom of the big hillside field and started to climb to the woods at the top of the hill. Benteen went with him.

They went up the hill beside a stone wall. Trees grew out of the wall and other trees grew beside it, but on either side the land was open: on their side was the big hayfield, across the wall a rocky pasture. Away on their left, two miles off, the steeple of the church in the village could be seen, behind it the new stack on the steam board mill at the edge of town. From top-of-the-woods you could see the roofs and chimneys of all the houses in the village.

When Benteen and Vergil had set out for the hill, the first yellow daylight had lain at their feet in long angles across the ground, cutting through the blue grass like a blade, but now it seemed to be on toward noon. Vergil went a little ahead. Somebody had given him a clumsy summer haircut. His hair was cropped close to his head and high, off the back of his neck and up above his ears. It made him look like a chicken. His hair was blond. Vergil's dark pants were held up by suspenders that crossed his back in a big X, and his legs and back, bent a little into the slope, carried him up the long hill without effort. Benteen felt the hill more, but he would make it all right.

Some way up they came to a crew of people sitting under a big old oak tree that spread over the wall like a tent at a summer fair. There were four or five of them. They had been mowing the field, it seemed, for they had two mowing machines waiting out in the open, in the sun, along with a wagon, while their horses were fed in the shade of the trees: two horses for each mower and two for the wagon, six horses in all, standing in under the tree with the men. They were resting as though they had spent the morning cutting the hillside, but there was no sign of mowing, nor was the grass very long. They didn't pay much attention to Vergil and Benteen as the two went by them. They sat in a row with their backs against the wall, drinking from time to time from a white china pitcher they had and fanning themselves with their straw hats. One of them, Benteen saw, was a girl or young woman, the others, men. He didn't know any of them. He didn't know what they were doing out there. He didn't know what they were drinking.

Vergil stopped short of the top of the hill. Often it was when you first went into a little woods like that one that what you were after, the squirrels, the rabbits, would start and reveal themselves for the only time, so you had to be set. The woods covered a few acres at the top of the hill. They were thicker, darker, at their edges than in the middle and so they formed a kind of ring around the hilltop.

Vergil opened his brother's .22 and slipped in a shell.

You'll never hit a rabbit with that thing, Benteen said.

Not looking for rabbits.

What, then? Benteen asked. That big fellow? You think that big fellow might be in there? Are you going for him?

Vergil looked at him. He shut up the little rifle with a snap and put the hammer on half-cock.

That? Benteen said. You hit that big guy with that and all you'll do is make him mad, he'll run right over you. You ought to see the size of him. You ought to see the size. You ought to see—

But Vergil turned and started toward the woods.

Hold it, Benteen said. Wait. Look, you can use my gun. I got it. You can't shoot that big guy with a .22, but you can with mine. Here. Here it is.

Let's see it, then.

He had it in his hands. He had brought his rifle, or his father's rifle, the one from London that looked like a plumbing fixture with a fancy stock, the elephant gun. Benteen had it in his hands, but now he'd lost Vergil. He'd come into the woods, making his way through the scrubby firs that grew at the edge, and now he waited, standing on the dead leaves and fallen branches of the interior of the woods. He couldn't see Vergil but he knew where he was. Up ahead, right at the top of the hill where the woods thinned out, was a spring of cold water that came up from the rocks and filled a little pool. Vergil would have gone there for a drink after that long hot climb from the yard. It was likely they'd find that big fellow in there, too; he wouldn't stray far from water. Benteen thought he could see him right now, ahead where he knew the spring to be, moving through the trees, an enormous thing, tall and silent, like a moving wall.

Deputy Rackstraw parked his cruiser beside the gas pumps at the Texaco on the edge of the village and went in to use the bathroom. He put water on his face, washed his hands. He bought a Pepsi-Cola and a bag of potato chips from the kid who worked there, left the station, and returned to his cruiser. Hugh was sitting in the passenger's seat waiting for him.

"Huh?" said the deputy.

"Don't shoot, Mister Deputy," said Hugh. "Get in. Here, I'll hold your soda."

The deputy handed his Pepsi-Cola through the window to Hugh. He got in behind the wheel, started the engine. He pulled away from the gas pumps, made a turn in the road, and drove away from the village. When they were under way, the deputy glanced at Hugh, then he took the pistol from his right hip and reached behind him to put it on the back seat. Then he held out his hand and Hugh gave him his drink.

"You afraid I'll take your gun off you?" Hugh asked him.

"I'm not afraid of anything you could do," said Deputy Rackstraw.

"You could have killed me with that thing the other night," Hugh said.

"That's right," the deputy said.

"Got the windshield instead, though, didn't you?"

"It looks that way," said the deputy.

"What did that cost you, a whole windshield?" Hugh asked.

"Four hundred," the deputy said.

"Four hundred?" said Hugh. "Shit, that's harsh. Is that your treat, or does the office get it?"

"The office," said Deputy Rackstraw.

"Line of duty, I guess, right?" said Hugh.

The deputy didn't answer him.

"We need to talk," Hugh said.

"No, we don't," the deputy said. "I've been looking for you two days. Now I found you. We're going to Brattleboro. We're going to get you processed down there, get you into a cell down there. We don't need to talk at all. If you want to talk you can talk to the public defender down there. He's about as full of shit as you are."

"Talk to him about what?" Hugh said.

"About what?" the deputy said. "Well, about grand theft. About that little horse cart, there, last month. About that weather vane. Other stuff. About your faggot friend in Boston. About Terry. There's lots to talk about."

"You're not thinking it through," said Hugh. "Ask yourself what it is you really know. You know you were out at Benteens' Monday night. You know you saw somebody coming off the roof of the barn. You know he ran away. You know you took a shot at him. You also know it was pitch dark. What you don't know, not for sure, is who he was. You never got close enough to see."

"I know damned well who it was," said the deputy. "I only wish I'd put one right up your ass so I could have had a body to show instead of this."

"Yeah, that was tough luck," said Hugh. "Then you'd been alright. As it is, though, I bet you couldn't even get them to charge me."

"You just told me I could have killed you," Deputy Rackstraw said.

Ahead of them the road divided, the right fork being the back way to Brattleboro.

"'The other night,' you said," the deputy said. "'You could have killed me the other night.' You just said it."

"That was for us," said Hugh. "Between us. That's what I meant. We need to talk private. You know? Informal. Between us. I know I got a problem here, too. See, I know that. We both need to talk."

Deputy Rackstraw slowed his cruiser and brought it into a turnaround beside the intersection of the Brattleboro road. He stopped under the trees and shut off the engine.

"That's the stuff," said Hugh. "Keep your eye on the bird, here, Mister Deputy. Think about your objective, here. Think about what it is you want. What you want is for me to be gone. Ain't that about it?"

Then the next morning, about the same time, somebody else is banging on the door and of course I thought it was Buddy back, although I'd understood they had an arrangement by then even if I didn't know what it was. He'd done something else and Buddy was after him again because of it, that's what I thought at first when they started in at the door, but no, it was her, very much lathered up and her hair not combed, wouldn't come in. He's gone, she said. I went to sleep and now he's gone.

Well, he ain't here, I said. He ain't with me. God's sake.

Course I knew what it was, it was Garrett, and for a second I had to laugh because, goodness, here with him and Buddy and the state police, and now Garrett gone off the deep end—I thought, What is this, some kind of a sale on trouble this week?

What happened? I said.

Well, she'd kept watch the best way she could, but it was so long. He had slept from after dinner Monday, when they brought him in, all through Tuesday, and all Tuesday night. She'd lain down in her room after midnight Tuesday thinking to nap but she'd slept for five, six hours. And when she woke up around six and looked in, he was gone. She looked all over the house, looked around outside the best way she could. He's nowhere there.

No, I said. He'll have gone back to the woods. It'll be like the other day but worse. We better get Marv.

Wait, she said, there's more.

She'd looked into his book room, looking for him, and found the gun cabinet in there was standing open and she wasn't sure but she thought one of the guns was gone. Not but what she'd ever taken much notice of what guns were in there in the first place, but she thought one was missing and certainly there was a place for a gun in there and no gun to it.

Oh, I said. Oh, I don't like that. We better go get Marv.

Well, she said, she'd gone to Marvin's right off for help, but nobody was there.

Course not, I said. He's haying, isn't he? He'll have been out since first light. You missed him.

Where is he, then? she asked.

Well, I don't exactly know, I told her. One of three or four places, could be any one of them.

Isn't Hugh with him? she asked. She didn't know that part, it seemed like.

Uh, not today, I said. Marv might be at long fields, I said. He might still be up on top-of-the-woods.

Shoot, she said, I don't know where any of those are.

Course you don't, I said. But I do. Come on, we'll go. I'll drive. We'll find him.

So I put on a sweater because it's cool these early mornings now, and we got in my car and started out for long fields because it was nearest. On the way I had to laugh again. I said to her, Listen, what is this? You lost track of Garrett, so you come looking for him at my place? At 6:30 in the morning? God's sake. What were you thinking?

*V*ergil stood beside the spring. Benteen was behind him. It was all wrong: somebody had laid the spring up square and cut and cleared all around it. Hemlock trees and alders had grown beside it and kept it dark. Water bugs moved over the still surface. The pool at the end where they stood was three feet deep, and there the bottom was white sand. The sand stirred faintly with the currents of the springs that fed the pool. Farther out the bottom disappeared and the pool grew deeper. Why was it all laid up like a tank, then? Why was it cleared out all around?

I don't know what we're doing here, do you? Benteen said. That big guy isn't here. He won't be here. This is farmland.

It sure ain't.

This is farmland, Benteen said.

Vergil didn't answer him. Instead he took off his shoes, stripped his clothes down in a pile, and walked naked into the spring.

Hey, said Benteen. Vergil walked out to a place where the water was above his waist and waited. His back was to Benteen. Benteen didn't know how he could stand it, for the water was so cold it might stop your heart, but Vergil didn't seem to mind it. While Benteen watched him, he put his arms together in front of him and fell forward into the water, going under toward the deeper side.

Hey, said Benteen. Are we hunting or are we swimming? But Vergil had gone into the water.

And, indeed, Benteen saw that big fellow was still there, after *all. It passed among the trees on the opposite side of the spring, but it was moving away, going away from him toward the back of the hill where it would go on down the other side to the brook and the road. They would lose it then.*

In the middle of the water, Vergil came to the surface in a rush and a splash that made the whole spring pitch and roll like water in a tub. He pushed his butchered hair back with his hands, turned to face Benteen, the water running down his neck and chest in rivers and flying from his arms in spray. For all his health and hardiness, Benteen saw, Vergil wasn't a big man. He had light-boned arms and a narrow, white chest; but still his body could do everything he needed to have it do, and he was altogether the kind of skinny fellow who is tough as a whip and lasts a long time.

Come on, Benteen called to him. Come on. He's going. He's getting away.

You go on. You take him. I'm staying.

We found Marvin at long fields. He was mowing clear at the other end. I stopped and she got out and began waving to him, and I beeped the horn. He saw us right away, but would he put up his sicklebar and come straight back down the mowing? He would not. He kept right on just the way he was, cutting, and we had to wait while he came all the way around to us. He stopped and switched off the tractor and sat and let us come across the cut hay to him. All the time in the world.

She got to him first. She told him Garrett was gone, had been gone for several hours maybe.

All right, was all he said. But he got down off his tractor.

We were all in a hurry to go, but no, before he was ready he went to the toolbox on the tractor behind and took out a plastic bag and put it over the seat. You know, here's his boss run off goodness knows where, in trouble, maybe hurt, and he's got to make sure he don't get his bottom wet when he comes back out here to finish the job.

We went to my car and on the way she told him about that gun that Garrett might have taken. He didn't say anything at all to that.

He wouldn't shoot us, would he? she asked him. We were in the car by then and Marvin didn't answer. He looked at me.

Cordie? he said.

Are you asking me? I said.

Well, when we got back to Benteens', Marvin said not to stop at the house and we went right on through the yard, around the barn, and down the cow track to the gate, as far as you could go in a car. Past that you get down to a brook runs below the pasture, then it's all woods going up the hill to the top.

I'd thought that was as far as I'd go, but when we got to it of course I went with them.

You might stay here, Marvin said. He meant both of us. There's no need for three to go up.

I'm going, I said. And she nodded, and so Marvin started out. We got over the brook on a couple of stones and went into the woods.

How do you know he's here at all? the girl asked.

I don't, Marvin said. He might be two places. I hope it's this one, not the other.

Well, I've got to start walking, riding a bicycle, getting some kind of exercise, I don't know, something. It's a long haul up there. There's a stone wall you keep on your right and you go up and up through the woods. Well, it's thick in there. You have to go over or around fallen trees, brush, branches, it's dark, it's damp, and the bugs are awful. It's like a jungle. But up at the top it kind of levels off and the trees are bigger and farther apart, anyway it's easier going. Marvin went first with her right behind him and me bringing up the rear. I was wearisome by then. Right up at the top there's a little spring of water.

Well, he wasn't there but his clothes were. That's right, his clothes, all of them, all dumped in a pile beside the spring: shoes, underwear, belt, all. I thought for a minute he'd gone into the spring himself and drowned, but there's no more than a couple of feet of water in there and you can see into all of it. He wasn't there. He'd gone on. Without a patch of clothes on him, seemingly, he'd gone on into the woods.

Well? I said to Marv.

But Marv is still looking into the spring, walking around it looking down into the water here and there. What is it? I asked him. He ain't in there.

No, Marv said. I was looking for the gun.

"You're joking, my boy," said Mr. Guest.

"No joke," said Hugh. "I signed up Friday. Me and Dudley Doright went in together, he saw me do it. That was the deal. I got to report tomorrow."

"Where?"

"Boston Government Center," Hugh said. "They put you on a bus for North Carolina, South Carolina, some fucking place."

"It seems extreme," Mr. Guest said. "I can't believe it's for the best."

"Yeah," said Hugh. "Well, it seems a little extreme to do five years in St. Albans, too. That's what I was looking at, you know. I could have the Marines or St. Albans. You know what they do to you up there—the other guys? You know what they do?"

"Well, put it that way and I suppose you're right," Mr. Guest said. "And, as to that, there's no war on, after all. Not like my day. They were a pretty tough party in my day."

"The fuck they were," said Hugh. "You were a Marine?"

"No, no, my boy," said Mr. Guest. "Intelligence. Stayed on, actually, 'til '47. Splendid bunch of fellows we had. It quite gets in your blood, you know, that work. Spoils you."

"I could have handed you to them, you know," said Hugh. "I could have given you to them and walked away—no St. Albans, no Marines. Free ticket."

"I know you could have," said Mr. Guest. "Of course, you didn't. You never would have. You're a gentleman, my boy. I must say, you fill me with hope. I'm going to miss our collaboration."

"They know all about you, you know," Hugh said. "If you don't quit it they'll get you. They're close."

"I hardly think so, my boy," said Mr. Guest. "I'll go on, and they'll go on. I'm an old dog. They'll never reach me. They don't know how. And if ever they should learn, if ever they should get too close, well, perhaps I'll simply move up here to Vermont and disappear, forget about the world."

Marv rolled the clothes up into a bundle and we started back down to the car. About halfway down the hill, I couldn't go on, I had to stop. Flopped right down on that stone wall so I could hold my hand up against my side.

Marv and her stopped and came back for me.

Are you going to make it? he said.

I was puffing. Yes, I said. Yes. But not right now. You go on ahead.

No, Marv said. Best we stick together. Is your side hurting you?

Some, I said. I just got to sit a minute more.

We waited then, not long. In a minute she went on. I was sitting on the wall under this great big tree that grew kind of like an umbrella over and in and around the wall there, the wall went right in one side of the tree and came out the other, and all around more woods, right close in. Dark. It was like sitting in a closet, except when you stopped crashing through the woods the way we had been, you could hear birds all around you in the trees.

We got to get on, Marv said.

I'm ready, I said. The bugs were eating us all up as it was, and the rock I was sitting on got real hard real fast, so I was enough uncomfortable resting to be ready to go. Marv got me under the elbow on the side that hurt and he was going to help me along that way, with his hand under my elbow. That girl is out ahead of us, moving pretty fast back down.

Get off, I said. God's sake. I can make it.

You'd thought he was getting ready to take me into a dance. We're both a little old for that kind of thing.

Well, we got back in the car, got turned around, and drove back through the yard and down the lane to the road. Marv drove. We went left. Marv's leaning right on it now, we went fast.

Where are we going now? she asked him.

Condostas' job, Marvin said.

We came to the place under the hill where they'd been cutting all summer, and there in the clearing is Terry Condosta's truck with the sign on the door, but nobody around. Well, Marv didn't even much slow down. He swung past the truck and started for the track that went up the hill, there, nothing but mud and rocks but it looked like we were going to take it in the car. My car.

Hang on, Marv said.

We went up the hill full throttle, bouncing and bumping along, slipping and banging around in the mud, but we made it to the top, only there we bottomed out hard and the car died. My car. And as soon as it did we heard somebody shouting up ahead. Marv was out of the car and walking toward whatever it was, not running. She and I followed a little back of him.

The first thing I saw was Terry Condosta with his white cowboy hat. He had his back up against one of his logging machines and his hands were up in the air and he was yelling something and what he was yelling at I first took for a bear or some giant I don't know, monkey, but it was Garrett. He looked brown or kind of gray, all over dirt, or mud, really. Not a dime of clothing on him, soaking wet, and with a rifle in his hands that he had pointed right at Terry, right at his chest. He wasn't yelling. He wasn't saying anything at all. He was standing there naked as a baby, dirty like that, muddy, and he was all cut up, slashed and scratched all over his body, I guess from tearing through the woods like that, and he was shaking, shaking and shivering, but he held the gun and he had it right on Terry. Between them was a cement cellar full of green slimy water. Garrett was at one end of it, up on the cement rim, and Terry was backed into his machine at the other end.

Well, Terry was carrying on: Get away from me, you crazy (I won't say it). What do you want? You crazy, I'll have you locked up forever. You're trespassing. You get away from me.

His voice was way high. He was scared and when he saw us he showed it.

Bland, Terry yelled. Get him off me. What's he doing? What's he want? Don't let him do it. Don't let him shoot. Jesus. Oh, Jesus Christ, Bland.

Like that.

Marv stood there for a second and then he walked right over to them.

Shut up, now, he said to Terry. Terry shut up. Marv got between Terry and Garrett, with that gun looking right at him. I have to say it took a certain amount of courage, because I don't know if Garrett knew who he was, or who we were, or where he was, or much of anything else. Marv walked right up to him and he said, Come on, now. It's over. We got to get back now.

Well, Garrett, like I said, is soaking wet and he's cold. He's shaking so bad I was afraid the gun would go off. He kept it right up on Marv's chest the whole time, two inches away.

Come on, Marv said. Come on, now.

And I heard Garrett say something like, He's in there. He's in there and he won't come out. I can't get him to come out.

He put up the gun and handed it to Marv.

I know, Marv said. Let's get on back. Might be he'll come out when we're gone.

So soon as he handed over the gun, Terry was out of there. He didn't say a word, just started walking fast back down the hill. Did he give me and her a look when he went past? He gave us a look because we women had seen how scared he'd been. Well, who wouldn't have been? He and Hugh are friends. Were. They went to Dartmouth together but Terry graduated and is doing well. You heard of doing too well? I wish he didn't have to wear that hat.

Garrett had kind of collapsed, sunk down onto the concrete rim, there. Marv laid the gun to one side and got down with him. The girl went to them and got down on the other side of Garrett and they were kind of supporting him and

Marv said to me, You want to give us a hand over here? Well, there he was in his skin like a big drowned muskrat, the way I said, but worse, much worse.

God's sake, Marv, get some clothes on him, can't you? I said.

Marvin drove Hugh to Brattleboro to get the bus for Boston. They left in plenty of time, but five miles out of Brattleboro they came to a wreck. A trailer truck had gotten across the road and turned over. Police and the fire department were waiting for a wrecker to come that was big enough to clear the truck. Until it arrived the road was blocked. Marvin and Hugh waited with a dozen others.

"If I don't make it I'm fucked," Hugh said. "This ain't like missing the previews."

"Well, we can wait here or go around the back way," Marvin said.

"That's going back the way we came," Hugh said.

"I'd rather that than sit here," Marvin said. "But you decide. It's you that's got to be there."

"Shit," said Hugh. "Go for it."

So Marvin got them turned around and they went back up the road to Ambrose for several miles, then turned east, went over the river and by back roads working southeast to Brattleboro the long way. If there were no more trouble they ought to make it.

"She'll be moving on," said Hugh.

"Not what she says," Marvin said. "Says she's staying."

"At Garrett's?" Hugh asked.

"She says."

"No," Hugh said. "She'll move on. She'll have to. She's got nobody left to protect her from her boyfriend. She'll have to leave. Unless you're up for the job."

"Not me," said Marvin.

"You think she'll go?"

"No," Marvin said.

"What about her boyfriend, though?" Hugh asked.

"What about him?" Marvin said.

"Well," said Hugh. "What do you think, she's going to sit out there and hold Garrett's hand, feed him his soup, while she waits for that guy to bust in?"

"Says she is," Marvin said.

"No," said Hugh. "Never happen."

The Boston bus was boarding when they arrived at the depot. The driver was climbing to his place. Hugh would have to run.

"She can't be going to stay," Hugh said. "It makes no sense, not for her. What's she get? You know what they're doing out there, don't you? Nothing. They talk. They sit and talk. What's there for her, then? We both know it ain't the pay."

"You best get moving," Marvin said.

The doors of the bus closed and its brakes released that hiss.

"Go ahead, now," said Marvin.

"Fuck it," said Hugh. "Here I go."

He jumped from the truck, swung his bag out of the rear, and ran for it. The bus was rolling, but the driver saw him, stopped, opened up, and Hugh got on.

The end of it was I wound up with a son in the U.S. Marine Corps, off someplace in the South, on account of a deal he made with Buddy Rackstraw and some magistrate. I didn't know anything about it until it was done. I said, You're doing what? You're going where?

I got it then. The deal was enlist or get arrested right then and there, get tried, and maybe go to jail for stealing from Benteens'.

That was you? I said. You stole Garrett's little cart?

Stole a lot more than that, he said. Thinks he's something, even now with this. What a bonehead.

Listen, I said. I'll go see Garrett. Garrett might let you off the hook, here, he might not what do you call it? I'm sure he wouldn't want you to, you know, go to jail. Prefer charges.

You'll go see Garrett? he said. Garrett's in the rubber room. He's under lock and key. You know that. Nobody's seeing him. Anyway it don't matter, he don't have to prefer anything. I made the deal. It's done.

Okay, I said. That's it, then. Give me a minute, here. Okay. Okay. How long do you have? When do you have to go?

Thinking, of course, that he'd have a couple of weeks at least, I mean, going off to the Marines and all.

In about an hour, he says.

What? I said. When? Oh, Lord.

Well, I sat there like a fool and then Marvin drove up, and he gave me a kiss and a hug and he picked up his suitcase and he was gone. And after a while it occurred to me to think, Wait a minute, who did you say thought up this deal? Buddy? Or you.

I wound up with a boy in the Marine Corps and Garrett wound up with her. Well, he's got to have somebody out there now, he's about knocked in and it will take time, it looks like. Doctor seemed to think he might have had a little stroke along with everything else. It looks like if you've got to tear your clothes off and go crashing through the woods trying to shoot somebody, you'd do it when you're young enough to get over it if you live. Garrett has had the radish. But he'll be back. In his own way, Garrett's pretty tough. The other day he and her turned up out at top-of-the-woods watching Marv and LeRoy load the last hay. Just watching them from the barway. Marv and LeRoy waved, and he waved back.

With Garrett laid up, I don't suppose people would draw the same conclusions now from her living out there that they did before—though I don't know why not. Anyway, there she is and there she'll be. Is she taking some kind of survey, here? I mean, she's on her way to getting around the whole town—traveling on her back, too, just like a little sea otter. Did I say that?

Well, it's a three-year commitment with the Marines and I truthfully wonder if he'll be able to stick it. I said once to her how his idea of authority was that you can't flap your arms and fly like a bird, and I don't know how somebody like that is going to take to something like being in an army. But it's done and it looks like he'll just have to stand it. At least there's no war on. And after it's all over, who knows? Maybe he'll come back here and take up where he left off. Maybe he won't. For now, it looks as though he was always busting to get out of here, to go someplace else, anyplace else, and now he did it. But not quite the way he thought.

What occurs to me is it's once more like Daddy used to say. He loved to say this. He said take care what you want for you will by God get it.

Tyler poured a shot of brandy into the cup of coffee she'd made and carried it out of the kitchen and onto the porch.

"Who was that with Marvin and Boomer?" she asked.

"That was LeRoy," Mr. Benteen said. "Marvin needs help. He's got to get it done before the weather changes."

"LeRoy," said Tyler. "LeRoy. Another one of your hands, is he? Another one of your men?"

"That's right," said Benteen.

"What's this one stolen lately?" Tyler asked him.

"Nothing I know about," Benteen said. "Did I shoot at him? I mean, did I fire that thing?"

"No," Tyler said "You kind of pointed it at him."

"What did he do?" Benteen asked.

"He was yelling at you," Tyler said. "He was begging. Then when we came and you gave up the gun he got out of there fast."

"I bet he did," Benteen said. He shook his head. "What was going on?" he asked her.

"If you don't know," Tyler said. "Nobody else does."

Benteen shook his head again. He took some of the coffee.

"You helped this a little," he said.

"A little," Tyler said. "How do you feel now?"

"Not too bad," Benteen said. "Tired, some. My legs are shot. Being crazy don't hurt your head, you know. It gets you in the legs. Did you know that?"

"Not 'til now."

"It's a fact," said Benteen. "You could learn a lot out here."

"We both could," Tyler said.

"I'm a highly unstable fellow, though," Benteen said. "You're out here with a highly unstable fellow. Also highly old. Considered from your point of view it don't look to me like much of a bargain. What do you think?"

"I think you're right," said Tyler. "It's not much of a bargain."

"No," Benteen said.

"But I can handle it," Tyler said.

"I don't doubt that," said Benteen.

"I still want a lock, though," Tyler said. "I still want a lock for my door."

"And I still ain't going to give you one," said Benteen. "No locks."

"What about Hulon, then?" Tyler asked. "You're all knocked out. That boy's gone. Everybody else is helping Marvin with the hay. And I can't even lock my door. What am I going to do if Hulon comes?"

"No more about Hulon," said Benteen. "No more about him, now."

"Why not?"

"Why not?" said Benteen. "Because there's no such fellow. That's why not."

"There isn't?"

"Isn't. Never was. Never will be."

"Are you saying I've been making it up, about Hulon?" Tyler asked him. "Are you saying I made it all up? All this time?"

"That's right," said Benteen.

"Are you calling me a liar?" said Tyler.

"I am."

"Well," Tyler said. "I wondered who it would be around here that finally figured that out. I didn't think it would be you. I thought you were crazy."

"I'm crazy," Benteen said. "I ain't stupid."

"How did you know?" Tyler asked him.

"About Hulon?"

"That's right."

"Nobody's name is Hulon," Benteen said.

"One's is," Tyler said. "Hulon Dangerfield. Ford dealer this side of Waco. He was partners with my father once, for a while. That's where I got the name. It's a long story. Do you want to hear it?"

"No," said Benteen. "No time for a long story. Story's about done."

"I guess it is," Tyler said. "In a way, I don't like to see it end."

"One thing," said Benteen. "What happened to your head? When you came here you had a lump like a hen's egg. I saw it. What was that if it wasn't him?"

"I told that boy," Tyler said. "I ran into a door."

"Is that right?"

"Don't you believe me?"

"I don't know," said Benteen.

"It was a door," said Tyler. "Listen: would I make up a thing as dumb as that?"

"I don't know."

"You want to know what my Daddy used to say?" Tyler said. "He used to say: If you got to lie, tell the truth but change one thing."

The same afternoon he finished cutting at top-of-the-woods, Marvin's tractor quit. He left it up there. Then it rained for three days, and blew, so after that they had a job to get it all in, all the hay, with LeRoy, who came in for Hugh, and Boomer taking off from the inn to help. As it was, they lost a good part of it: when it comes off cool and wet that late, with the summer getting done, you're going to lose some.

So he'd never fixed the tractor. He hadn't had time. It sat out there at top-of-the-woods with a tarp over it and it was into September when Marvin got out there again. Then he got it going, barely, and drove it down through the woods to the road. When he got it onto the road, though, the tractor began to act like it was getting ready to quit again, so Marvin stopped at a pullout to look it over. It was there that Marco Condosta, driving by, found him. Condosta stopped and backed his car into the pullout beside the tractor.

"You're out of luck, here, I guess," Condosta said.

"Well," Marvin said. "It did pretty good to get down from up there."

"These old things, the timing belts will give you trouble," Condosta said.

"They will," said Marvin.

"You got tools?" Condosta asked.

"Not for that. At the shop I have."

"Get in," Condosta said. "I'll drop you."

"I don't like to take you out of your way," Marvin said.

"I was driving around," Condosta said. "That's all. I don't do much any more. I'm semiretired. My boy takes care of things. I stay out of his way, you know what I'm saying? Go ahead, get in."

So Marvin got in beside Marco Condosta, who took his time turning around and starting back toward Benteens'. He drove slowly, with his head held far back and his chin sticking up in the air, looking down his nose through little glasses. Probably he couldn't see.

"How's your boss?" Condosta asked Marvin.

"Coming," Marvin said. "He's coming."

"Good," said Condosta. "I never see him. I told him once, the same thing: 'This little place we got here, and I never see you one year to the next.' I hope he's doing okay."

"He'll be all right," Marvin said.

"You'll tell him I was asking," Condosta said. "I was sorry for all that, back there, but you know how it is. Terry's running things now. I just, well, I'm semiretired. I don't do much. Tell him I was asking."

"I'll tell him," said Marvin.

They drove into the yard at Benteens', through the yard to the barn. There Condosta stopped the car and Marvin got out. In the barn, above the big doors, the loft was open. You could see the hay bales stacked in the loft, a solid wall, more bales stacked under canvas covers beside the barn, still more, also covered, on the high hay wagons standing in the yard. Walls of hay, houses of hay, a city of hay.

"Boy," Condosta said, "you made a lot, didn't you?"

"We made more than this," Marvin said. "We lost, oh, load and a half when it got so wet."

"I know," said Condosta. "It cooled down. It still is. It won't come back. I put a jacket on this morning. I was driving up past Stratton earlier, just driving. Trees up there are turning."

Marvin nodded.

"Fall," Condosta said. "Before you know it it will be winter. We'll be up to here in snow."

"Thanks for the ride," Marvin said. "One of the others can take me back out."

"Winter," said Condosta. "Do you do anything? I guess not."

"Do anything?"

"You know, go anyplace? Get away? Where it's warm?"

"No," said Marvin.

"We've been going down by Sarasota," Condosta said. "The last two years. No, three years. We got a little place down there now. Go right after Christmas, stay 'til, I don't know, the middle of May. We thought, why not? It's alright."

"It sounds nice," said Marvin.

"It is," said Condosta. "It is nice. I don't like it, but it's nice. You know what I'm saying? It's alright. Listen, you got work to do. Tell your boss to take care of himself. Tell him I was asking."

"I'll tell him," Marvin said.

Condosta drove on past the barn, turned around, and left Marvin standing in the yard as he went by on his way out. He waved to Marvin. Marvin waved back. Then he turned and went to the shop to find what he needed to fix the tractor. That day an end-of-summer noon, the air blown out clean and the sky as high and keen as a steeple with those big white clouds like freight cars going by, but up in the real mountains a few leaves are turning, the old men always the first to spot them and bring the news.

I am persuaded that everyone goes into his life with one particular talent of his own, one gift, and this is mine: I never gave a damn what anybody thought of me. Short of going through the world as a scoundrel, as some kind of shitheel aristocrat, I have gone my own way and lived as I pleased. Anyone who thought I was a drunk, a madman, a rich trifler, was welcome to his opinion. The first two I certainly was, but I was never as rich as they thought.

My mistake was in thinking that if you held onto the old land and some of the old ways you could hold onto the old life. It don't work. If you got to buy it it don't count. Because the land isn't the life, the ways aren't the life. You have to hold onto the men. You have to hold onto the men and they won't let you. Not even your own. Not any of them. They will find a way to kick over. You can't run them unless they let you. All the fuss we make about a free people, liberty, government by the consent of the governed. Course. How not? What the hell other kind is there? What other kind could there ever be?

Here they come. This is no drill. They're coming in waves, in floods, by the millions, more and more each year. They are coming up 91. We made them a straight highway and now they have got to have a place to go. They have got to have a place to go and this is it. They will spread the little towns out until they bump and join, they'll build new towns. They'll grade down the hills, blast them away with dynamite, until their city fills every crack and corner like black floodwater. It will happen, nothing can stop it. And when they've finished the building, before they've finished, they'll knock it down and build it all over again, higher, darker, louder than before. It's their life now, and they will have it. Nothing can stop them, or if something can it's not what I had: it's not money, and it's not care.

Marvin, my good old friend, I understand tore the bottom parts out of Cordelia's car in the process of keeping me from committing mayhem on Judgment Hill. Obviously, that one was on me. I paid over the money easily, even grandly, and not without a rueful smile. She tells me I put my gun down on that young fellow 'til he about soiled his drawers. Did I? I suppose I did. I wouldn't have shot him. Or maybe I would. One thing: that old cannon would have made quite a hole.

Now they tell me the ram on top of my barn is a fake made out of aluminum siding. When, they ask, am I going to get rid of it and put the real one back up there? I'm not sure I will. Let the fake one stay up there and let everybody know it's a fake. Leave the fake in place and let them like it.

They will. From down here you can't tell the difference anyway.

In a minute I'll get up and go. I'll go out and about, see what's doing. No hiding. Anybody who thinks I'm still dangerous, anybody who thinks I ever was, can god damned well get out of my way, I won't chase him. The fall's coming, the best time of the year, the time when you can see the machinery of the year, see the big wheels slowly turning. Best time of the year—a time out of time. That's it, yes. For a couple of weeks in the fall it looks like everything will always be the same, keep coming around the same way, forever, the same turning. In the fall you can almost make yourself believe that nothing really changes, but it ain't so and in the end, whether you like it or not, whether I like it or not, it's the way I told that beauty, that handmaid, that stranger, that driver, that fatherless child, that female traveler done with traveling, it's the way my educated brother, my own father, told me even years ago: If the country goes to hell, or if it goes to heaven, Vermont is going with it.

M arvin laid the barrel of Mr. Benteen's rifle across the stone wall and got right down behind it, putting the front sight on the shadow in the brush in front of him, but when at last the creature itself came from the thicket into the opening, he took in his breath and sat up to look at it.

It was tall, black, its flanks streaked with a kind of rustiness like the sides of an old iron ship, its spreading antlers the size of a hammock rigged above the great head, which moved among the middle branches of the bare, gray trees.

That's bigger than it was summertime, said Marvin. A lot bigger.

The great creature was reaching its long neck to crop winter buds among the trees. Its eyes were closed. It moved through the trees on slender, delicate legs like stilts, as long as stilts.

Could there have been two of them and this is the big one?

It never made a sound. As big as a ship, it went in perfect silence. Now it had come out of the last trees and stood no more than twenty feet from where Marvin hid behind his wall and pointed Benteen's .505.

Well, I got to do it now, said Marvin.

It moved again, showing its full left side to Marvin. He couldn't miss now; it was like shooting a house. He got down again, found the sight, held his tongue between his front teeth, took in a breath, cocked, and fired.

Marvin got him. He heard the very bullet land, land on bone—a horrid sound like a well-hit baseball—an instant before the blast of the shot. But the creature didn't fall, didn't react at all. It went on nipping the twigs, flicking its long ears from time to time.

I know I got him, said Marvin. I got him with a gun for elephants.

He cocked the other barrel and fired again. Again the nasty *whock* of the solid hit and the huge, ringing *bronngg*. Still the great beast didn't move, was unhurt, but now it left off browsing in the little trees and turned its head toward Marvin. Nothing could kill it. He saw the big round eye turn in the head, round and brown and indifferent or even benign, perhaps, but nevertheless full of danger, like the eye of a horse who is about to kick you into the next township.

I best get out of here, said Marvin.

He stood and with the creature watching him he backed away from the wall a few steps. Then he turned and, carrying the rifle, walked quickly toward a dark stand of little pines that was nearby. In among them he stopped, looked behind him, and saw the animal still waiting where it had been, looking after him. While Marvin watched, though, it forgot him and went back to its browsing. Then it took a step, then another, and moved easily off into the woods.

Where are you going to? Marvin said.

I set out to write *Judgment Hill* hoping to produce a kind of written landscape-with-figures, a picture, at first simply of the look of the southern Green Mountain foothill country as I have come to see it. My picture would be no real picture, however, but a work of fiction, and therefore it would rely not on description but on a story. That story I would make up, as I would make up everything about it: its people, its speech, its pleasures, its pain, its hills and houses, its cats and dogs, its weather. Just because *Judgment Hill* would not be a real landscape but a narrative, it would, I hoped, take on more completely than most pictures can a mental or moral life of its own and so give the reader a way into its subject matter: time and change, fortune, friendship, love, memory, and the mysterious, elusive past.

I find I haven't quite written the book I expected to write. You never do, I think. That's why you write them in the first place. That's why you read them.